The Sleeping Bears of Leelanau County

THE SLEEPING BEARS OF LEELANAU COUNTY

Paul Wcisel

The characters in this book are entirely fictional. However, the locations and establishments are places the author has visited and thoroughly enjoyed while living and traveling in Michigan.

First edition December 2019

Book design by Paul Wcisel
paulwcisel.com

Independently published
ISBN: 9781676439448

To Michigan

CONTENTS

And the mountain said, "*Don't worry about me. I've been around long before you were here. And I'll be around long after you're gone.*"

– A Conversation with Nature

INTRO

We were in the secluded woods outside the town of Cedar, waiting for our killer to arrive. This had not been the Michigan summer I expected.

"Do you think he'll arrive soon?" I asked. It felt like it was taking longer than it should.

"Don't worry about the timing, Max," Hannah replied, sensing my anxiety. "I'm guessing another five to ten minutes, although he is a little late."

We were waiting for Bern who had faked his death for the cameras. They orchestrated the whole show—the sheriff, local journalists and several county officials were part of the network. It was all a ploy to send the media and excitable hunters back home. Our members handled the convincing close-ups. *They'd gotten the bear, the killer, and here was the proof.*

In the past it would have been much easier to pull off a lie like that, but in today's invasive world of lights, cameras and surveillance it took diligence. I had been an accessory, watching the "victim's" last moments before the fateful attack—and it was terrifying. Bern mauled him with a vengeance.

And now here I was with Hannah, standing with a backpack of shoes and clothing waiting for him to emerge at the designated meeting spot. "He's nearby," she said, "I can smell him." Moments later Bern ambled up to us still in bear form. It was much easier navigating the forest that way. A 300-pound black bear walking right at you was something I used to reflexively caution. Now, like Hannah, I was utterly calm.

Bern stood up on his hind legs to transform, and though I'd experienced it frequently, it was still eerie to witness. In a blur he was standing there naked, reaching out, asking for the backpack.

Slipping in and out of the spirit world didn't apply to material items like clothing and jewelry. Those ended up dropping to the ground during the instant you transitioned. It was better to be bare (bear?) while making the change to ensure you wouldn't lose something or accidentally shred it.

"Looking good, Bern," quipped Hannah with a glancing observation. "Great acting. Very credible."

"Thanks," he replied while putting on the clothes. "They drugged me up a bit so I'd really look the part. Diazepam, Valium, whatever they call it these days. I'm feeling pretty mellow. I thought the gunshot wound to my neck was worthy of a Hollywood make-up artist."

He'd been transported by the others while the drugs wore off. They let him out along County Road 616. The autumn foliage had yet to fully arrive and there was plenty of green canopy for cover.

"Apologies for the slight delay. I paused to snack on a few patches of black chokeberries along the way. I couldn't resist. They were perfectly ripe." Bern had a wry smirk on his face. "Let's hope that will be the end of it. The entire episode was *executed* perfectly. Pun intended."

1

A Blue Tattoo

I arrived in Leelanau County with the intent of enjoying the
beaches, biking trails, kayaking waterways, fishing clear rivers
and lakes, and exploring the quirky bars and restaurants. What I
didn't anticipate was discovering a completely twisted perception
of the world. Or maybe I should say I encountered the reality we all
sense but never fully understand.

I should back up and give that some context.

I'd been out of college and living on my own for a couple of
years but my hometown life had gotten stale. That summer I was
between jobs with no clear career path ahead of me. Minneapolis
was alright but I'd never seen a Great Lake other than Superior. My
plan was to road trip through Michigan, do some seasonal work,
and then turn south for the winter. Maybe I'd get to Tampa or New
Orleans. It didn't matter. I needed new scenery. Like the saying
goes: *If you don't change what you already know, you'll stay where
you are.*

My carriage of choice was an old Volkswagen Westfalia
Camper with a hitch for my road bike. Not exactly glamorous
but efficient, mobile, and inexpensive lodgings for the farm hand
work I had applied for. My first destination would be through the
Upper Peninsula, over the Mackinac Bridge, and down along Grand

Traverse Bay to a hop farm and orchard just west of Lake Leelanau. I would never get further than that. On the map it looked idyllic with bays, inlets, lakes and parks. Turns out that wasn't entirely natural.

As springtime rolled in and the last of the snow piles held out in shadowed patches, I prepared to load up the Westie and have the basics serviced to avoid future breakdowns. Oil change. New wiper blades. Fluids filled. Tires inflated. Brakes— good enough. Same for the shocks. It's a Volkswagen not a BMW. I wasn't going to be driving this thing in the snow. It's meant for meandering. Zero to 60 in one minute. My wardrobe was practical. Jeans, work boots, layers, nothing fancy. I wouldn't be dining at Michelin star restaurants or attending any ballroom dances. And of course a bunch of useful accessories like a fry pan, thermal mugs, spices, hot sauce, a sharp knife, a Swiss army knife (with corkscrew), water bottle for the bike, cribbage board, deck of cards, extension cords, collapsible cooler, backpack, fishing tackle, a two tin plates, coffee pot (a necessity) and two luxury items: a small rice cooker and compact toaster. You'd be amazed at what you can cook with those two appliances. Want some warm flour tortillas? Heat them in the toaster. Instant satisfaction.

On D-Day—departure day—I was up early at 0-dark-thirty. The drive to Marquette, the Upper Peninsula's largest town, was going to take hours. I would be staying at the Marquette Tourist Park for two nights. I had enough in savings to cover expenses and even a few disasters for the entire year. Any work was only going to extend that.

The drive out of town was luxurious with few other travelers, flashing yellow lights and the eventual sunrise to aid waking me up. I cruised into Wisconsin, passing through Eau Claire and Wausau before heading north along US-51. Unsurprisingly, it felt a lot like Minnesota, especially the lake-riddled region between Rhinelander and Eagle River. *Rhinelander*—now there's a fine, inexpensive beer. Before crossing into the U.P. I fueled up in Land O'Lakes. It was still early in the day and the town was quiet. I nibbled on a cinnamon Pop-Tart and pushed on through to my destination.

The Marquette Tourist Park is just north of the downtown. It's the typical sort of arrangement of RVs, campers and tents spread out between pines, with recreational attractions all within a short walk or bike ride. I pulled into my spot and started to unwind. I was hungry. The drive was long and it was about noon. Nothing sounded more appetizing at that moment than a burger and fries. I figured I'd take my bike into town, grab a sandwich and a beer and see what the place was all about. I locked up the Westie, got the bike off the rack, took a moment to get my bearings, and pedaled out, almost immediately finding myself on the campus of Northern Michigan University. Maybe I'd meet a few current or recent former students like myself while in town.

I rolled down 3rd Street. The weather was perfect, the sunny warmth of late spring thawing out the town. I settled on a no-frills sports bar called the 906 next to an old theater. The lunchtime crowd was fairly busy. I grabbed a seat at the neon-lit bar along with my growling stomach.

"Afternoon. What can I get you?"

I did a quick scan of the tap handles. "Oberon. And a menu." A slightly older couple two chairs over were passively watching a baseball game. They were bikers, judging from the riding boots, faded jeans and weathered jackets. He had a salt and peppered beard and looked like the type of guy who enjoyed a good time. She wasn't a stereotypical biker chic but an attractive blond—and she knew it. And so did he. Or maybe I always felt people like that exude an air of freedom and confidence that enhances their visual character.

The bartender handed me a menu and the beer. Oh, that tasted like summer! And the burger menu was exciting, if there could be such a thing. Make it a *906* by adding a third quarter pound patty? Tempting. I ordered, "I'll have *The Miner* with fries, please."

"You can't go wrong with the burgers here," I heard indirectly. "They're the best in town." The voice was coming from the blond biker.

5

"I hope so," I turned to answer. "I've been traveling all day and haven't eaten anything except a Pop-Tart."

"Well, you won't be disappointed. Where are you from?"

"Minneapolis. I'm on my way to Traverse City for a seasonal job," I mentioned, referencing the largest town near Leelanau County. "But I've got a couple days to tour the U.P. Despite the proximity, I've never been over this way."

And so the conversation started rolling. I filled them in on my wandering plans with expectations of ending up someplace warm for the winter. They charmed me with U.P. travel suggestions: Muldoons Pasties in Munising, Miners Beach, Tahquamenon Falls, Big Spring, Castle Rock, The Mystery Spot if only to say you've been there. Turns out they were partial nomads, spending at least a month every summer touring with their Harleys. They lived outside of Detroit and had made excursions all around the Great Lakes including places in Minnesota I was familiar with. Hank had his own plumbing business, the sort of occupation that is always in high demand. Lynn was a Realtor and apparently a very successful one, a fact that her biker persona misrepresented entirely.

The sensational burger was long gone and we had a few more rounds. I mentioned my bike and they suggested taking the lakeshore path out to Presque Isle Park. "It's beautiful. It'll be a great ride on a day like today. And have a nightcap at The Wooden Nickel Bar on your way back to the campground." That nightcap turned out to be the most prophetic suggestion of my life.

They got up to leave and were heading over to some place called Foggy's in a town called Christmas. "You can cook your own steak. We usually split one," said Hank. Lynn followed-up, "Nice meeting you, Max, best of luck with your summer. By the way, your burger and beers are on us."

"Thank you!" I exclaimed, caught off-guard completely by their overt kindness. And as I watched them exit the bar I thought to myself, Hank, you are one lucky bastard.

***

With a full belly and a pleasant buzz, I decided to make the ride up to Presque Isle like they suggested. I rode downhill to the lakefront harbor dominated by the huge ore dock—not that I knew what it was at that time. It's an enormous structure protruding out into the bay looking like a gothic bridge to nowhere. It's no longer in use but the even larger, more recent version further up the trail still is. The dock is several stories tall allowing for rail cars full of iron ore to spill their contents down pocket chutes into the holds of a waiting freighter. The sound must be dreadfully loud.

The loop around Presque Isle Park, which is really a peninsula, was exceptional. Beautiful vistas, rocky shorelines, small cliffs and crashing waves. At times I felt like I was looking out across the Pacific. Despite the sunny skies, the water was still super cold at that time of year. I watched a group of intrepid teenagers leaping off the short cliffs into the water like they were on a mission of great importance. "Holy shit, that is cold! Ahhaaaaa!" The shock of the water was followed by an immediate swim to awaiting towels. After an excursion to a scenic viewing point, I decided to head back towards town to see what this Wooden Nickel bar was all about. It was only about a mile from the campground so I figured I'd have a couple more rounds and call it a day.

I locked my bike to a street sign outside and walked up the steps into what felt like an old saloon. The Wooden Nickel had the vibe of a place that catered to travelers and locals alike, is what it is, and didn't give a damn if you had a jaded opinion about it. There was plenty of room at the bar so I ordered up another Oberon and took in the surrounding oddities. A pool table. Bubble hockey. Street signs, license plates and faded photographs. A deer skull and life preservers. Yes, this would do just fine.

Scanning the crowd I caught the eye of a stranger watching me from a table nearby. I looked back into my beer and then turned her way again. Still watching. I gave a sort of nod and a smile and she got up and walked my way. She was cute and casual — not that I'd expect fancy in a place like this — short black hair, a pullover

7

sweatshirt with a hood, converse high tops and torn up jeans. "Hi, I'm Blue." Reading my quizzical look she added, "Spelled like the color. I'm not describing how I feel. My parents told me my name was inspired by the lake."

"Have a seat, Blue. That is an unusual name. Not that my name is all that common. I'm Maximilian but everyone calls me Max."

She extended one of her heavily tattooed forearms to shake my hand. Her sharp nose brought focus to rather stunning green eyes. Yes, this too would do just fine.

"Can I buy you a drink?" I asked. "Karma says I'm due to pay back my free lunch earlier today."

"How about a beer. For now," she added suggestively. "You don't seem to be from around here. So, what brings you to Marquette?"

"Traveling through. Heading to Traverse City for some seasonal work. I'm staying in the Tourist Park for a couple nights. I actually just got into town this morning. I started out in Minneapolis." It already seemed like a week ago. "What brings you here?" I asked.

"I just wrapped up school here at NMU and then it will be on to something else. I've been curious about Seattle. Or maybe even Alaska." And she left it at that. "Care to shoot some pool, Max from Minneapolis?"

"Sure."

"Hey, Jimmy." Blue knowingly called out to the bartender, "Can I get two shots of tequila and some quarters for the pool table? The decent stuff, not José Cuervo." Jimmy the bartender gave her nod, "Gotcha," and ambled over moments later with the shots and a few bucks in quarters. "Industry discount," he stated and didn't follow up asking for payment. "Watch yourself, buddy," he directed to me, "she's a bit of a shark."

We tipped glasses, downed the shots, nodded at each other and

8

headed over to the table with our beers. The rest of that night is like trying to recall scenes from a movie that you watched through a broken mirror.

She *was* pretty good with a pool cue. I had a several decent rounds during that early peak of drunken relaxation when the game just starts to align. She'd bump me out of the way. We'd lean around each other in feigned interference, all of it an excuse to get closer, touch, check each other out. And after a few more drinks we were new best friends, commenting on a shared enjoyment of the music selections, watching others come and go, occasionally playing as a team against other patrons.

I don't recall paying the tab when she proposed that we go to her place. Blue lived a short walk from the bar, I believe in the direction of where I'd parked the Westie. I gave no thought about my bike locked to the street sign. Her apartment was on a second floor corner unit with a rounded window extension overlooking a dimly lit street. I remember it being fairly bohemian as you might expect with a student. A large comfortable sofa, an open kitchen, books, a mattress on the floor in the corner and lots of plants.

I mentioned being hungry and she grabbed some bread and honey from the kitchen. "Sorry, Max. My kitchen isn't well stocked. But you'll love this honey. It's magical."

Yes it was, because there was more to that honey than what the bees added.

Euphoria set in. I felt unattached, confused, yet calm and completely wonderful. "What's in that?" I probably asked. I recall her laughing while she was taking my clothes off. And then hers. She had tattoos all over but they were very botanical and natural in design. Butterflies, birds, insects, plants, vines, flowers. They danced and pulsed across her body in a hallucinatory manner. I was drawn deeper and deeper into the patterns and into her. Snippets of honey-induced ecstasy. We were lounging on the mattress. Is that jazz playing? More honey, why not? Blue naked, walking past the sofa to get us something to drink, looking like a breathing jungle landscape. Is that a bear in the apartment? God damn am I high. Blue are you seeing anything like this?

I distinctly remember the needle. She was tattooing a small blue square below the knuckle of my middle finger. Her signature, I think she called it. But the magical honey knew no pain and made me completely agreeable.

**

I woke up around noon to the sound of a dog barking and found myself lying naked in the Westie.

How the hell did I get here? Where are my clothes? Shit, my wallet and phone. I pulled myself up to assess my predicament. No worries. My clothes were all folded up nicely with a note.

Max -

Sorry I had to leave you like this. I had a great time. There's more to you than you might ever realize. I'm moving out west but perhaps we'll meet again someday. Think of me when you look at that tattoo. Where you're headed it may come in handy with the people you meet.

You're a good guy. Take care,

– Blue

ps. Don't forget your bike.

What tattoo? Oh, Jesus, I thought as looked at my left hand. What else did I do? But nothing seemed worse for wear. Everything was there. Money. Phone. All my belongings. And surprisingly I didn't feel hungover, although I wouldn't say I was feeling chipper.

What an introduction to Michigan, Max. You've got to get yourself together. Take this as a sign to move along.

2

An Unexpected Encounter

I located the campground facilities, readied myself to face the day, and mapped an escape route out of town. It was early afternoon. My fellow campers were long gone or out pursuing other activities. The barking dog owners had taken the little Jack Russell for a hike to the lake. As with my arrival, my departure went largely unnoticed as I idled through the pitched tents and trailers. I picked up the bike and snapped a photo of The Wooden Nickel soaked in daylight. It was a stark contrast to what I'd experienced only hours before. Motorcycles lined the parking lot today. I was tempted to go back in to see if Blue was in there but I thought better of it. I felt like a male mantis that got away with mating without having the female devour him. Let it be.

I drove east through Christmas, a small town where all the streets have names like Santa Lane, Pine Tree Road, and Mrs. Claus Lane. I passed by Foggy's, the roadhouse Hank and Lynn went to, and continued on into Munising. What appeared to be a house on a curved stretch of road was a sign advertising Muldoons Pasties. I pulled the Westie into the little parking lot and figured that would suffice for breakfast.

"What kind would you like?" asked the woman behind the counter.

"Um, I'll go with the veggie," I answered. I wanted something substantial but not so much as to be nap inducing.

She handed me a warm pasty straight from the hot cabinet. I'd had them before. Think of a giant empanada. "Ketchup and other sauces, napkins and utensils are right behind you," she added.

Now, Yoopers—residents of the Upper Peninsula—claim that ketchup is the best, but I prefer sriracha. Other people say only trolls put ketchup on their pasties. Whatever. I took mine outside to one of the picnic tables and devoured the flaky goodness in minutes. Damn if that isn't the best! I considered going back inside for another but figured the law of diminishing returns favored not being a glutton.

Fueled up, at least physically, I continued south to Route 2 and followed the shoreline of Lake Michigan to the Mackinac Bridge. Finally, I got to see another Great Lake. Sorry, Mystery Spot, but I'm not stopping this time.

It was a great drive but all the while residual memories from the night before would flash into my head. Blue and I dancing in her apartment. She's telling me something but like a dream it remains unclear. I glanced at my hand upon the steering wheel. How is it that my tattoo has already dramatically healed? It doesn't look fresh at all. And Blue's note, "It might come in handy with the people you meet." How would a small mark on my finger be helpful and what kind of people would give a damn?

Driving across the Mackinac Bridge was like a time warp. From point to point they say it's five miles long but you get so entranced by the stunning view that it seems to go by in a matter of seconds. Something similar happened last night but I couldn't put my finger on it, not even the one with the new tattoo. Blue and I returned to the campground and the Westie but not in a conventional sense. It was almost like we just... walked there? No, that's not it. And why wasn't I wearing any clothes when I woke up?

I took the scenic route toward Cross Village and stopped at a place called the Legs Inn, a restaurant with a cobblestone exterior and mannequin legs lining the roofline. Evening was setting in and suddenly I was tremendously tired. The night before had caught up to me completely. I decided to stay for a meal and a drink. *The Old World Sampler* of Polish cuisine could not have been more perfect and afterwards I passed out in the Westie parked on the street across from an art gallery. The hop farm and orchard in Leelanau County would be an easy drive tomorrow.

That night I dreamt I was walking with Blue through a forest, or was it the campground back in Marquette? But we moved along like animals, undetected and familiar with the elements. It felt like it actually happened, but of course it didn't.

I woke up feeling refreshed but in need of a shower. Hello, Lake Michigan. I strolled out to a dock and jumped in with a bar of soap and Oh My God is that water cold. Quickest bath I'd ever take in my life. Fortunately there were no onlookers to mock my icy decision. I toweled off, scurried back to the Westie, tossed on a flannel and continued on my journey, passing through Petoskey, Charlevoix, Elk Rapids, eventually rounding Grand Traverse Bay while cruising through Traverse City. "Now, here's a town with some nightlife options," I thought, observing the bustle of activity.

I headed down Front Street and doubled back to have breakfast at a little dive called J&S Hamburg. That's hamburg, not hamburger. Sitting at the counter was like a trip back to a simpler time. Domed pedestals offered red velvet, chocolate, and carrot cake. My fellow diners, locals no doubt, were griping with the waitress. "They're going to tear up more of what makes this place special just to put in another hotel and parking garage so the FIBs and tourists can have a weekend of fun." I sipped coffee, waiting for my breakfast to arrive and listened to a consistent theme: expensive rent, expensive housing, low wages, and rampant development.

I was curious. "What's a FIB?" I asked.

"Fucking Illinois Bastards. You know, the people from Chicago with money to burn," was the reply. Apparently this Michigan paradise had been discovered and now people were up in arms about the intrusions and slipping sense of community. Kids were selling the home mom and dad left them to the highest bidders and leaving town. Short-term rentals were introducing a new flock of strangers every week. "You won't even recognize the Leelanau Peninsula ten years from now," they said, citing the development and changes that already transformed Old Mission Peninsula from open space and farmlands to subdivisions and mansions.

Later that morning I finally made it to my destination, the hop farm and orchard just west of Lake Leelanau. Introductions were made and my employers were kind enough to let me hook up the Westie to a small farmhand residence with luxuries like a bathroom and shower with warm water. It was designed to be a communal residence but I arrived early, so for the time being it was just me.

After a week, I established a routine of hard working days followed by biking excursions along the beautiful trails in The County—which is how everyone in Leelanau County referred to it. Life was going as expected. I discovered the awesome and hilly Heritage Trail, stopping for lunch in Glen Arbor before returning to Empire. Along the Leelanau Trail, there were gems like Hop Lot or Little Bee's Italian Ice in Suttons Bay. And that trail extended through Traverse City as the TART, winding along to the East Bay.

But my new life was far from tranquil. At night I had continued dreams of what I considered "Blue Events." Animal wanderings. Shape-shifting landscapes. I felt haunted, like when you know you've forgotten something but can't remember exactly what it was or why you needed to do it.

***

It was an overcast May afternoon, and I was having lunch at the Cedar Tavern, when I overheard other workers talking about augmenting their income by making way more than my hourly wage selling morel mushrooms by the pound. "Sign me up," was what I was thinking. That would be much more lucrative than trimming brush and readying the orchard. "Where can I find these mushrooms?" I asked. I figured I'd get a helpful tip. After all, the sign above the tavern entrance proclaims *The Best People In The World Walk Thru This Door*. "Around," was the vague reply. And that ended up being the catalyst for discovering my mentor, friend and new employer.

On a Saturday afternoon, I had wandered way off the beaten path searching rotting logs for telltale signs of the unique fungi. A large pileated woodpecker sounded off, hammering away at a birch tree. In the distance, across the trillium-covered forest floor, I noticed a fellow mushroom hunter. She was far more successful and carried a huge collection of morels in a large sack. I had yet to find a single mushroom and I knew my intrusion would not be welcomed. Yet, I felt compelled to call out so I didn't come off as some sort of stalking asshole. "Hello, there!"

She turned and took a quick assessment of me as I approached. "I sensed someone was following me." She had that natural, attractive look of someone very active in life who stayed fit and could care less about makeup. She was wearing hiking pants with a pair of well-worn work boots, a heavy flannel sweater and a mess of unkempt blondish hair. I can picture it like it was yesterday. I had no idea how incredibly transformative this woman would be in defining my future. Meanwhile, I must have looked like the complete novice that I was, holding an empty sack and gawking at her full one.

"No, no, no," I assured her, "I just saw you and didn't want to scare you unexpectedly."

"Oh, that's very kind of you to do so," she answered a bit sarcastically. "Really I can take care of myself."

I bet she could, I thought. She continued, "You're not from around here. I've not seen you before."

Apparently I'd bumped into one of The County's more established residents. "You're right. Hi, I'm Max. I'm doing some seasonal work at a hop farm west of Lake Leelanau. I've been here just over a week and decided to try hunting for morels. Seemed like a quick way to make some cash. Clearly I've not figured out how to find them," I said, indicating my empty bag. I extended my right hand.

She started to say, "Yes, I surmised you were…" and then tapered off into silence and stood frozen for a moment, her gaze fixed on my left hand holding the empty bag. "That's an interesting tattoo you have. Where'd you get it?"

My eyes shifted over to the tattoo. The little blue square appeared strangely brighter, almost alive.

My face probably expressed my own momentary puzzlement. "Oh, that's a recent acquisition. I got it up in Marquette. It reminds me of the water." I decided to leave out how I got it. After all, I wasn't entirely certain.

With a quizzical look she studied my face. "It's rather unique. Marquette, huh? Well, anyhow, I'm Hannah," she took my hand. "Welcome to Leelanau County."

I don't know why I said my next few words but they changed my life forever. "Nice meeting you, Hannah. Yes, the tattoo artist had the name Blue. I feel like she put a bit of herself into the color."

I half smiled, like I was saying something clever. Hannah practically fell backwards.

"You got that from Blue?" she exclaimed with a louder, knowing voice. And then, as if to believe it herself, she said it again definitively, "You *did* get that from Blue."

Now I was nervous. Here I was in the woods talking to an excitable stranger. What had been a normal introduction became something cascading off the rails. "Um, ye yes," I stuttered. "That was her name." I stepped back. Would I have to defend myself?

"Oh my god," Hannah was shifting from bewilderment to joy. "She had a bunch of tattoos herself, didn't she? Short. Dark hair.

Maybe green eyes?"

Now I was dazed. Yes, she knew her alright. What were the odds of that happening? Better to just roll with it.

"Evidently you know each other," I answered as calmly as I could.

"Listen, Max Whatever your last name is. You're coming along with me." Hannah said it like an executive decision. "I have to hear more about this but let's talk elsewhere. I can't believe you met Blue!" She was grinning.

Saying no wasn't going to be an option.

I don't know what it is about the women in Michigan, but ordinary is not the term I'd use to define them.

And so began the first of my many forest hikes with Hannah.

3

WELCOME TO REALITY

As Hannah and I walked back to her car she continued with questions, first asking more about Blue than myself. "Where in Marquette did you meet her?"

"A bar. She mentioned being a student at NMU."

Hannah laughed at that. "Well, at least that's what she told you. She certainly isn't a student. But I completely believe the part about the bar. Did she mention any plans?"

"She said something about going to Seattle or possibly even Alaska," I replied. "We started drinking tequila and beers and it got pretty out of hand from there."

Hannah raised an eyebrow. She was probably at least 15 years older than me but had the looks and qualities of someone living their life much younger. "How outta hand do you mean?"

I wasn't sure how to answer. Here was someone who appeared close to Blue but my mind started clicking off possibilities. Mom. Sister. Aunt. "Please don't tell me you're related?"

"No worries. No, not in the conventional sense," answered Hannah, picking up on my reservations. "Let's just say she has a way of being a bit more than she appears."

"You got that right," I said.

Hannah's Subaru was visible along the roadside. She had a bike rack and I suddenly remembered my bicycle stashed off a path locked to a tree. "Hey, can we pick up my bike? It should be down the road off a path. I'll recognize the trailhead."

"Yeah, no problem, Max." Her saying my name already had a comfortable familiarity. "We'll head back to my gallery in Glen Arbor. We've got to finish this story and I'll cook up some of these morels. Where are you living now?"

A free meal was all the invitation I needed. "On Walker's hop farm and orchard. Eventually some other seasonal farmhands will join me. I've got an old Westfalia Camper. It's not luxurious but I'm outside most of the time anyway."

"Walker's aren't one of us but they're good people," Hannah responded.

One of us? What did that imply? I wondered as we hopped into the car. We drove a few minutes along the winding, empty stretch of road and I retrieved my bike.

Getting back in Hannah continued, "So, how'd that night with Blue end up going?" Her bemused expression indicated she already had an idea. I loosely translated the stream of events from that night without being specific. Meeting at the bar, playing pool, heading back to Blue's apartment, the honey, the music, the tattoo, the blackout return to the Westie and her note.

We turned into Hannah's driveway and parked in front of the single-car garage. Tall pine trees surrounded her place giving it a screened seclusion apart from the rest of the business district. Her backyard opened up to the woods with no immediate neighbors. During the drive she seemed to be calculating my story like a sudoku puzzle, piecing it together to reveal a greater clarity.

Her ranch-style home and studio were small but completely efficient, each with an open floor plan and a large, sliding industrial doorway between them. She sold ceramics, jewelry and other artwork alongside her workspace. Her apartment was eerily similar to Blue's with the open kitchen, sofa, and lots of plants, but Hannah at least had an actual bed and also a small corner fireplace.

"These could sell for $50 per pound," she indicated, pointing to her bag of morels. "Usually I supply the restaurants around town but you're arrival calls for a special occasion. Care for a beer? I've got some Short's, Bell's, and I also have some excellent mead from St. Ambrose."

"I'm a fan of Bell's," I said and she handed me a Two Hearted Ale, grabbing one herself.

Hannah started to melt butter into a large cast iron skillet. "I've got some fresh asparagus I'll cook up, too." And she paused, "Max, where did you say you're from?"

"Minneapolis," I answered.

"Okay. I think I've got this but I'm not sure. So, did Blue tell you about being part of the clan?" she asked.

"What?" I replied. "Fuck the Klan."

Hannah almost spit out her beer laughing. "No, not the bed sheets and pointy hats! *Our clan.* That's why she signed you with that tattoo. I get it now. You're in hibernation and have no idea."

What the hell was she talking about? "I'm sorry but I don't follow what you're getting at," I stated.

Hannah turned off the stove and grabbed a seat across the table with me. "Your night with Blue, did you happen to see any bears?"

My wide eyes of disbelief at the accuracy of that guess answered for me.

Hannah continued, "Ah, so you did. Did you ever feel like you were changing?"

I started to get the chills. Goose bumps were rising on my arms. "How are you guessing this? What do you mean by hibernating? Blue gave me some psychedelic honey, I'm pretty certain we got naked and danced to some odd jazz music. But it's really all a blur. I'm not sure what happened."

Hannah could sense my anxiety. "Take it easy, kid. That helps. FYI the jazz was probably Miles Davis *Kind of Blue* or Coltrane's *Blue Train*. She likes to be funny like that." Her voice was soothing. "Max, I'm going to tell you something fantastical and then prove it to you it's real, but you might want to have another beer to take the edge off." She got up and got us another round but remained standing like a teacher in front of a classroom.

"You're part of a genetic clan although you're parents probably never knew about it, either. Our clan's spirit animal is a black bear." She was watching to make sure I was tuned in. "There are two worlds existing in parallel balance, side by side. The one you can see is the material world around us. The other world, some cultures refer to it as the invisible world, the spirit world, nirvana, a heightened sense of reality, a vision of clarity. We—members of our clan—have the ability to slip into that world and return as bears."

My sideward glance must have indicated my skepticism.

Nonetheless, she continued. "Blue is what we call a spirit bear. She can easily see both worlds and travel extensively between them. That magical honey was otherworldly, wasn't it? Well, that's because it is. A few weeks ago Blue started on a journey to find out if there were more of us outside The County. Obviously there are, but she could easily spot hibernating clan members like yourself. Talk about a cosmic harmony! She knew she wouldn't have time to mentor you—that's really not the role of a spirit bear anyway—so she gave you her unique signature, knowing you were heading here, and figured someone would take you in. Looks like that's going to me." Hannah shot me a pleasant smile.

But I wasn't so sure about that. We were strangers just hours ago and now she was telling me fairy tales. I tilted back my beer to avoid saying something rude and started to consider an exit plan. My bike was still on the rack. I could run out.

"So, Max, got any questions so far?" she asked.

"Okay. Bears, bears, bears. Right. And how does one do that, the whole changing thing?" I asked with an annoyed overtone. This was ridiculous. Yet, the coincidence of her knowing Blue and our happenstance meeting in the woods kept me seated.

"When people in our clan mature, a feature in our brain allows us to transcend our spirit animal," she said matter-of-factly. "But it takes practice to understand the connection. Like a child learning a language or how to ride a bicycle. Get ready, I'll show you."

Hannah crossed to the front window, did a quick check outside and then drew the curtains. "Now, Max, remember. It's just me. I'll wink at you and wave to let you know." She started to remove her clothes. I began to get up, thinking should I leave—or come over?—but she motioned me back toward the table. "This isn't a come on. Please sit back down." I complied.

But it was alluring. Hannah was quite fetching with the body of an athlete, tone and trim. A natural beauty. I was starting to feel like an inadequate version of Benjamin from *The Graduate*. What a strange afternoon this is going to be, I was thinking to myself. It's incredible that I've been here only a week and already...

And like that she changed into a bear.

I don't remember but I must have jumped because I knocked over my chair and tumbled to the ground, the beer bottle slipped from my grasp and rolled around. I couldn't breathe.

The bear didn't approach but kept staring at me. Was it winking? Then it raised a paw and appeared to wave. Terror kept me frozen, lying on the floor like a broken statue.

In a relative instance there was Hannah again standing naked in the room. "You took that fairly well," she said. I was speechless. She started gathering up her clothes, getting dressed. I couldn't move.

"Max, the truth is you can do that, too. So, what do you say, want to learn more about yourself?"

I nodded, still stunned.

"Alright. Well, you'll have to tell the Walkers you got a new job. You can park your Westie here and work for me. I'll be your mentor. Deal?"

She gave me a reassuring hand, "Let's get back to cooking those mushrooms. Looks like you could use another beer and I'm sure you'll have a few less-sassy questions for me, now."

4

UNWANTED DEVELOPMENTS

M oving in with Hannah brought me into the greater
community of our clan. I'd work her gallery space during
the day while she gathered morels. It was evident that selling
artwork at the studio wasn't her main source of income but her
works were compelling enough to make an occasional sale. She
said custom projects for the big vacation homes in the area
provided some real money, along with foraging and supplying the
local restaurants with edible plants, mushrooms and wild berries.

At night she would to teach me meditations to help wake me out
of hibernation, saying it would be awhile before I caught on, to not
get frustrated, and let the persistence pay off. "How did you learn?"
I asked her one evening.

"My parents taught me when I was a teenager. They were very
active members of our clan. Instinctively the knowledge is there but
these practices are part of an oral tradition that goes back centuries.
I'm teaching you meditations that people have been using long
before there was a Michigan, even in its current geographical form."
Hannah's answer befuddled me.

It was a lot to take in. Had she not demonstrated changing into a
bear I would not have believed a word of it. Yet, here I was learning
about a dormant aspect about myself all because a stranger—I

mean, spirit bear—tagged me with a tattoo knowing with cosmic clarity that I'd be taken care of.

Hannah would occasionally close up shop to lead me out into the forest. She revealed that changing was a great way to cover ground and the heightened senses of a bear gave you a distinct edge over other foragers. Of course, you had to return to the locations in human form to gather the rewards. A bear paw isn't very adept at picking up and carrying things. That spring as we hunted and foraged, we'd return with bags of mushrooms and even I was capable of contributing despite not being able to transform into a bear.

One Saturday she announced, "We have to attend a meeting over at Dick's Pour House in Lake Leelanau. There's been another push from an outside developer threatening numerous acres in The County and we need a plan to counter that. It's an informal, get to know the situation sort of gathering. When we make definitive decisions for our clan we usually meet in private."

"What do you mean, don't you simply run through the usual governmental channels?" I questioned.

Hannah gave a wry smile, "Well... a lot of us *are* the government in The County. Our members include law enforcement, local officials, school boards, journalists and reporters. We've fostered a political climate where even residents without our unique bond also support maintaining a balanced environment."

Hannah continued, "Sure, there are a lot of natural resources here but we have been vigilant in maintaining them. And it's no coincidence that the area is desirable and relatively safe. After all, we're a human community. We value things like reliable roads, good schools, and access to conveniences like grocery stores. But we are extremely protective of our natural assets. It's not coincidental that Sleeping Bear Dunes National Lake Shore has that name and is here in The County. And the Leelanau Conservancy? We govern that as well and have been able to save some incredible pieces of land that, if developed, would turn this place into just another suburban landscape."

She was passionately delivering this discussion. How big of a reach did our clan have, I wondered? I had yet to consider the group as being so well organized. "So, is our clan statewide and national?"

"No, our clan keeps to this region. You can control a lot more about where you live by paying attention to local matters and representatives. Mostly we're in Leelanau County although a few members live just outside in Benzie and Grand Traverse." Hannah was sounding like a community activist, which in a way I guess she was. "However, we're not the only sort of people transcendentally linked to a spirit animal. There are other bear clans, wolves, deer, even smaller creatures like ravens."

I couldn't believe what I was hearing. Or I suppose I could. How had I been living in the—what did she call it—material world without ever knowing this?

"I can see from your face that you're finding this amazing," she teased, "like the first time a kid tastes ice cream. I'll tell you the full history of us at a later time, but consider it a rule of thumb that most anyplace where humanity is living in harmony with nature, then you're likely to find a clan involved politically, somehow. Typically we don't overlap our zones of influence. That can lead to pretty nasty conflicts although in some cities like Portland, Oregon it has worked out exceptionally well. Whereas in a place like Dallas it failed miserably."

"Could that be worldwide?" I pondered out loud.

"Maybe," she said. "I'm aware only of New World/Western Hemisphere communities but it wouldn't surprise me to learn of tiger clans in India, pandas in China."

"How does the whole resizing work?" I couldn't imagine it. "A person turning into a little raven. Come on." As if a bear made complete sense.

"I don't fully understand the specifics, kid." She often addressed me in ways that underscored my being so new to all of this. "Think of it like water. Under the right conditions it can be ice, liquid, or vapor, all with different properties and volumes. Split an atom and you produce a profound amount of energy. So, our clan has this genetic capability within our brain. And that's an organ no one understands completely. Personally I like to think of it as coal becoming a diamond."

"Anyhow, I'm rambling," she cut herself off. "Come on. Let's head to the Pour House."

***

That evening we met with other members at the renowned public house. A few tables had been pushed together and pitchers of Michigan brewed ales dominated the landscape. When we arrived, everyone greeted Hannah lovingly and eyed me with suspicion. In her typical manner, she broke the ice with a simple comment. "This is Max. He met Blue. Check out the tattoo she gave him." It was like having an all-access pass for acceptability. And I'll be damned if that little tattoo didn't appear to fluctuate in vibrant lake hues whenever I was around other "Sleeping Bears" as they would jokingly refer to themselves. OURselves.

"How's it going, Max?" I'd hear one of them say. "Grab a pint."

Hannah and I ended up sitting across from each other amongst a group of six other men and two women. The focus of heated discussion was a developer's plan to turn the south end of Duck Lake near Leland into a vacation destination unrivaled in The County.

"We lost the Homestead Resort," Finn was framing his argument, "and now these T-Rex bastards want to turn the real estate south of Leland into another playground for the rich. You'll have a golf course, run-off and wastewater polluting Duck Lake, Lake Leelanau, and Lake Michigan. Sleeping Bear Dunes will have bookends of irresponsible cottagers."

I'd learned that "cottager" was slang for a temporary resident, usually with inherited wealth, drunk most of the time, and arrogant with a self-absorbed sense of importance. T-Rex happened to be the shorthand name for Texas Real Estate Exchange, Inc., a real estate investment group—out of Texas, big like a dinosaur—known for ruthlessly buying up entire rural communities in desirable locations and converting them to Anywhere Vanilla, USA. The sort of destination where you don't really experience anything too dangerous or new, you just don't have to care about trashing the place because it's a rental.

Finn was gray and lanky with a shrill voice that served him well barking out orders on a boat. He was an older resident of Leland and ran a small charter fishing company out of Fishtown during the warmer months and spent his time drinking in the winter. Viewing his situation as an outsider, you would think he would welcome the prospective growth in business. But like Hannah he didn't give a damn about that. His community and way of life was already here and he enjoyed having neighbors who looked out for each other. To Finn's way of thinking, transient housing was like having the neighbor's dog shit in your yard and them not bothering to clean up after it.

"They'll never be able to finance that," Tom chimed in. "People have tried and we've always been able to stall and defeat them with zoning ordinances. Besides, there are some huge homes in that area that would never sell out. The Good Harbor folks in the region would have too much to lose." Tom was slightly younger than Finn but short and burly. He was also from the Leland area, a member of the Leelanau Conservancy, and was key in securing the Houdek Dunes Nature Area.

"Those owners *aren't like us*," Finn countered, underscoring the concern.

"Finn, you're being all crank bait about this," Hannah observed. "Tom's right. These ventures rarely come to fruition. And Finn, the Homestead people aren't all that bad. They've been good neighbors despite our initial apprehensions."

Before Finn could agree or counter, Bern interjected, "You've not experienced these T-Rex agents." That was the first time I heard from Bern. He was roughly Hannah's vintage and it was evident they had an attraction for each other. He had those rugged good looks that appealed to everybody and his presence always added value to a gathering. They shared a passion for the outdoors and all things local.

"They're cunning," he resumed. "They stay in short-term vacation rentals and try to dig up gossip and conflicts among the community they plan to extort. I've bumped into them at the Bluebird, Hop Lot, Northport Brew—or whatever they're calling it now—posing as friendly, inquisitive tourists. All the while they're armed with plat maps and public tax records attempting to leverage local disputes to their own advantage."

"That seems excessive but not surprising," Tom noted. "With available land forever at a greater premium the lengths some of these developers go to knows few bounds. Consider Traverse City: a majority of the residents voted against taller buildings yet there's constant pressure on city commissioners to allow for them anyway. It's a form of reasoning that profits no one but the builders."

"Well," said Bern, "the T-Rex guys are probably trying to influence whoever they can with cash, gifts, lawsuits and subtle threats."

One of the other women chimed in, "Gentleman, let's not get too excitable until we have more information." That was Kate, older than Hannah with salt and pepper hair but similar in appearing excessively healthy. "I'll see what I can learn from the area residents. I've heard that some of the homes with frontage along Lake Michigan have been approached and offered substantial sums if they'd sell but no one has jumped at the money, yet. Of course, maybe those offers succeed if the price is right."

"Or they dig up some dirt and blackmail the owners into selling," concluded Finn. "All this electronic data is convenient for the good, the bad and the ugly. It happens in business and politics all the time.

'Take this offer or you're family will learn about your affair.' That sort of thing."

"Luckily," Hannah followed, "we're a united front and always have been." She wasn't letting the conversation unfurl into chaotic speculation.

Over a few more rounds I met the others, all older than myself. They got to know my story, Hannah would fill in the gaps, and eventually the talk of the T-Rex matter switched to casual discussions about other recent events.

The group gradually departed one by one, saying hellos and greeting others on the way out, until it was just Bern, Hannah and myself at a single table.

Hannah put out an invitation. "It's still early. We can close this out at my place if you'd like?" Obviously, I was along for the ride but for Bern it meant something more.

He nodded in my direction, "But I though Max here was staying with you?"

"I've got my Westie parked alongside the garage," I offered. "Mobile comfort."

"Max has the studio space," Hannah clarified. "So, come on. I've got plenty back at the house and we can talk more candidly. Bern, you can leave your car. I'll give you a lift back here in the morning." Hannah's comment left me feeling like the definitive third wheel.

"Sounds good. I'll grab the bill," said Bern, getting up to pay at the bar. "Max, I'm looking forward to hearing more about your background and that encounter with Blue."

We all piled into the Subaru to head back to Hannah's. I didn't have to ask about Bern taking shotgun. It was evident he'd ridden alongside Hannah for a while.

5

LIFE WITH A SPIRIT ANIMAL

We were sitting around the kitchen table. Hannah and Bern had switched to drinking mead while I stuck to beer. One benefit of living with Hannah is she always had a stocked refrigerator and pantry full of local beverages and food due to her connection supplying restaurants with foraged delights. They would purchase supplies for the weekend rush and share premium items whenever she dropped by. But for our impromptu gathering she just put out some Leelanau Raclette cheese with some crackers. I can't recall tasting a better cheese anywhere else.

"So, Max, where are you from?" Bern was snacking on a cracker, talking to me but looking at the tattoo on my hand. Having a lost member of the clan show up with a signature from Blue wasn't an everyday occurrence.

"Minneapolis. My parents lived there all of their lives and I was an only child. It's a good place to grow up if you don't mind extreme cold and playing hockey," I said, describing the reality of life in Minnesota.

"I wonder if his folks were related to members of the lost tribes," Bern said to Hannah. "The location fits. It's right in line with the route Blue was considering."

"Well, according to Max, Blue is already on her way much further west to Seattle and possibly Alaska," Hannah replied. "I think she's looking to go way, way back to find out if there are any of us still in the old country, I guess one might say."

Old country? Lost tribes? What were they talking about? But before I could ask, Bern continued. "Are your parents still living in Minneapolis?"

My answer wasn't uplifting. "Unfortunately, my mom passed away when I was a teenager. Lung cancer. She was a closet smoker despite all the warnings. I guess it eventually caught up with her." I didn't feel that explanation needed to be much more in-depth. "I lived with my dad before heading off to a local college. While I was there he was killed in a multi-car pile up. White out conditions on a highway during a winter storm."

"Jesus, Max," Hannah said, "that's terrible."

"It is. But, so it goes. They weren't super wealthy. Being an only child I inherited their modest home and some savings—I suppose I should say, my dad's estate by then—but nothing substantial. I used it to pay off some student loans but never finished getting my degree. My head wasn't into it. I was sort of lost there for a time and then tried my hand at a few different occupations before deciding to make this journey. I needed to get away from it all. Change of scenery," I added. "And so I took off with my modest bank roll figuring I better do so now, while I can, before I get stuck in a rut."

Thankfully, before I could say more Bern changed the topic. "How's it been going here in The County?"

"Hannah's been fantastic," I answered honestly. "She's taken great care of me, set me up with a job, and has been teaching me meditations to awaken my spirit connection out of hibernation. I usually practice in the studio during the evening or morning. I think

I'm getting there but I'm not always too sure."

"Oh, you'll know it when you get there," said Hannah. "It's like one of those *Magic Eye* illustrations. You know, the ones that look like a mess of colored dots but if you stare at them long enough to let your eyes relax suddenly they reveal a 3-dimensional depth of silhouette images."

I knew of those illustrations and it was a good analogy for describing the ability to see what's been right in front of you the entire time. I had hoped it would be a quick learning curve but so far—nothing.

"And when you think you're getting close be careful with wearing clothes that you value just in case they don't slip far enough away," added Bern. "Bear claws snag fabrics easily."

They were so casual about it, talking as one might describe an afternoon walk through the neighborhood. "How was it the first time you succeeded and when?" I asked, directed openly to both of them.

They gave each other a look as if to see who would answer first. Bern took the lead. "My parents taught me when I was a late teenager. It's not something you can really pick up before—what would you say, Hannah—sixteen at the earliest?"

"Strange, the timing coincides with getting a driver's license," she noted with a grin, "but that's correct. Our brains don't develop the ability until around that time. Which is a good thing. You don't want children turning into cubs."

I hadn't given a thought to kids turning into bears and was glad to hear that wasn't an option. But the idea of having a conversation with parents about being able to change into a bear was too much.

"Isn't that awkward as hell?" I asked.

"Yes," said Bern, "especially if you're parents are split. Meaning, one has our make up and the other doesn't. And of course being a teenager is super awkward." He gestured with his hand indicating the obvious. "But the conversation isn't like sex education, be careful around drugs, don't drive drunk. You just start to *know*, both you and your parent or parents. It's as if the spirit world sends everyone the message—you're ready."

Bern went on, "In your case, being older but still in hibernation, I'd say neither of your parents knew they carried the genetics. If it weren't for Blue you probably would have gone through life blissfully unaware. Sort of like that *Matrix* movie," he smiled with the connection, "just that the reality isn't so *grizzly*. Or, I suppose it is!" He was laughing at his own pun.

"The first time I changed I was taking a moonlight swim in Lake Michigan," Hannah started, ignoring the bad joke. "My parents knew I was about ready. It was a late summer night out at North Bar Beach. Back then you had a bit more seclusion. Not like today with Google Maps revealing every treasure and off-the-beaten-path gem. It was a beautiful night and we went skinning dipping," she was recalling it like a fond memory.

"We?" I interjected.

"Him," Hannah motioned toward Bern with her head. Then she turned to him with a huge grin. "God, we were so young!" He returned the look.

You damn well don't appear very old to me, I was thinking but kept to myself. Could they possibly be older than I guessed?

"Anyhow," she continued, "it must have been the calmness of the setting that I finally was able to transcend. It was strange because suddenly I was swimming in this bear form." She started to chuckle, "Bern knew about it, but one moment here's his naked 'girlfriend' and then bam! Bear in the water!" They each started to giggle at the vision.

I sipped my beer and was taking it all in. Hannah noticed we all were near empty and got up to get another round and a few more crackers.

"You guys make it sound like the first time you have sex. A sort of life-altering experience," I said.

"It kind of is," Bern answered dryly, "but it's that way with anything, right? I mean, the first time you see an ocean or the mountains. The first time you hit a home run or run a 5k. It's the realization you can achieve something else as well. And like some of those things, it doesn't last forever, either."

"How so?" It didn't occur to me that the ability to transcend with your spirit animal would go back into hibernation, so to speak.

"It's an aspect of life just like any other. At some point you become too old to change. It varies. Some people give up on it way early, finding little value in having the ability. Maybe they have far stronger talents like being an exceptional musician or master craftsmen and could care less about being in bear form. For others losing the ability can be devastating and depressing. But we all go through that and thankfully it does happen. It would not be a good idea to have senile bears running about. It's not a super power anymore than finding out you're a math wiz or a fast runner.

"There are members of our clan who can no longer transcend but are still very much part of our community. For outsiders I suppose they may come-off as being a bit eccentric, knowing what they know. But it's not like we are bears first, humans second. We're people with, what I would call, a heightened appreciation for the environment and how good life can be when you don't fuck that up," Bern concluded.

Eloquence aside, Bern's input was enlightening because I struggled with not viewing hibernation as a kind of handicap. It was refreshing to realize it was as natural a part of me as anything else. I could relate to it being an attainable goal like simply walking 30 minutes a day. It's very easy to achieve if you apply yourself.

"So what happens when you come across a bear in the woods?" I asked.

This time, Hannah jumped in. "If they're one of our clan, we recognize one another just as you would recognize a friend walking along the sidewalk. If it's an actual bear," she said with a laugh, "we scare the hell out of them. *Freak them out entirely*," she added with emphasis. "It's as if they can sense that we are not quite right. Or maybe to them we appear as being ghosts. Whatever it is they practically jump out of their skin. I have to admit, I get a kick out of it. And it doesn't matter if you're in bear form or not. They. Just. Do. Not. Like. Us. I never have to take in my bird feeders worrying about bears eating the suet. Yes, our community creates an environment they can enjoy, but like any animal they know better than to be trespassing into unfamiliar territory."

"Oh, that's good to know," I said taking a slug from the bottle of Two Hearted. "I have to confess I was worried if there ever was some, uh, bear on bear activity going on."

"Gross, no," said Bern, "but being new to the whole concept it's a legitimate question. Still gross, though." His face was crunched up like he smelled rotting trash. "When you're in bear form it's not like you crave getting it on with animals anymore than you do, now."

"Ahem," Hannah intentionally cleared her throat. "Tattoo boy here did have a time with Blue. Of course he doesn't recall it. She brought out some of her honey."

I didn't need Hannah mentioning my exploits but Bern paused and looked to me raising one of his eyebrows. "Is that so? My, my, my. Max, you've likely already stepped out of hibernation with a little magical nudge from Blue. And who knows what you got into. But you don't remember it, do you?"

I ended up re-telling the story of my encounter with Blue to Bern. And although Hannah had heard it all before she listened in like it was a favorite song she could play over and over. They both had a similar reaction to that part about me suddenly waking up naked in the Westie the following morning.

"How do you supposed she got you there?" asked Bern, knowing he was going to supply the answer. "Blue isn't exactly a large, physical presence. In fact, she's rather short and there's no way she could move you if you were totally inebriated." He gestured with his beer bottle and demonstrated a woozy character. "It's very likely she hooked you up with your spirit animal using some of her magical honey and moved you through the spirit dimension, dropping you off in bear form at the Westie before getting you inside. That would explain the lack of clothing."

"What do you mean?" I was befuddled. "Moved me through a dimension?"

"Spirit bears can do far more than any of us common clan members can comprehend. Not only can Blue access her spirit animal, she can inhabit the spirit world in that form. And it's right alongside of this one. She probably took you on a shortcut down a path that only people like her can make." Bern lapsed into thought. "How incredible that must be. But she would have needed to dope you up with honey, like an anesthesia, to get you there."

It all made sense. The vague bear memories. The flickering recollections of walking through the woods.

"Ever notice how that tattoo of yours seems to change?" Hannah motioned, "that's part of her magic, too. People outside of our clan won't see that but to us it flashes like a diamond."

"So, you think I've already been woken up?" Knowing this was intriguing. If I could focus my meditations on that night with Blue I might be able to hasten the end of my hibernation.

"Yes, kid. Try to bring that out in your practice," said Hannah as if she were reading my mind.

It was getting late but we were engaged with the conversation.

Bern speculated, "You all up for one more round?"

"Sure, Bern," said Hannah indicating something more than another round, "bring it."

"So, what happens if you die while in bear form," I asked, "do you morph back into a human like those werewolf movies?"

Bern was shaking his head, "No. You definitely die but as far as the public knows you become missing person, number whatever. You end up in that other dimension. Death. And there's no coming back from that one."

He was certain like a faithful preacher. I needed clarification. "Why call it a dimension? Why not say you're just dead? Don't you live on forever in the spirit world?"

Bern paused, contemplating an explanation. "It's impossible to know, so we theorize. Some of the better concepts portray our existence like molecules. Consider water—H_2O—two hydrogen atoms balanced around an oxygen atom, thus creating the molecule. Or more accurately CO_2, two oxygen atoms exactly opposite each other around a carbon.

"The two common atoms represent the material and spirit worlds. The yin and the yang. They're held in balance by a third atom, and for our purposes we'll call that the death dimension. There's no existence without that. It's necessary for both worlds to exist. And while we share properties between the common worlds—in our case the ability to transcend with a spirit animal—there's no mutual relation with the death dimension. Once you die you're out of balance and gone in the other. Energy to be repurposed for another time."

"No one will ever understand it completely," Hannah added, "but it also helps to explain the presence of people like Blue. She's like an element, having equal properties of both the spirit and material worlds."

I was feeling like a student in the back of a high school classroom trying to understand chemistry all over again. Their description was helpful but confusing all the same. Feeling sleepy, I opened up another line of questioning that had been nagging me.

"You've known each other for quite a long while. Have you been married or anything like that?" I tried to indicate with a facial expression that I didn't care but was simply curious. "Is there a secret ceremony in the community?"

Hannah answered first, "No, we're not a cult. Our clan is just like everyone else. Okay, sort of," she allowed. "Bern and I have known each other for a long time and we don't see the point in the formality of being married. We could owe more in taxes, and that's about it. We share our time as we see fit, while keeping independent identities. It's not like employers are offering great benefits anymore. Those days are long over. So, why bother? If you love each other that's enough. Keep it simple. Society and reality don't reflect the populace accurately. It's a brave new world. Always has been. Our clan has been adapting to changes for a long time. Same can be said for our relations."

"I agree," I yawned, "and I'm tired. I'm heading to bed. Thanks for all the information, tonight. It was great meeting the others at Dick's. But for now I hear the mattress in the Westie calling."

"Okay, Max."

"Good night."

I left them sitting at the kitchen table, rounding up empty bottles. Yet, later that night, lying in bed, I could have sworn I'd heard animals—bears—running out into the backyard, romping off into the forest.

6

Transformative News

"Kate's dead."

That was the topic of conversation in the community the following week. "The reports say she was driving on M-22 south of Leland when she veered off the road and hit a tree. She wasn't wearing a seatbelt and broke her neck when she went through the windshield."

The problem most people had with that story, I learned, was that Kate always wore a seatbelt and having lived in the area all her life she new every twist and turn of the roads throughout The County. "Might have been trying to avoid a collision with a deer," was the accepted explanation.

I happened to stumble upon a more sinister reason.

There wasn't going to be a solemn funeral, she left no dependents behind, and her small, private estate was to be handled by a local attorney who was also one of our clan. She had been well admired around Leland and there was an outpouring of sorrow for the woman who many recalled as being proudly independent. It was strange to think I had just met her, albeit briefly, a week before at Dick's Pour House. Her obituary in the Record-Eagle mentioned a life well traveled to Central and South America, a few achievements in regional racing events involving running, biking and kayaking, fluency in Spanish, and being a talented carpenter. She was certainly not a desk-jockey or one to regret a missed opportunity. The community planned to celebrate her with an informal party at a later date.

As May slipped into June the summer finally started to emerge in earnest. The season would be in full swing now through Labor Day. My initial plans of being in Leelanau County for only a couple of months were starting to unravel considering my new awareness. I certainly wasn't going anywhere until I pushed through my hibernation no matter how long that might take. Meanwhile, I'd been gathering up morels with Hannah on a regular basis. You'd be surprised how much money those mushrooms could bring in. And though you could gather them indefinitely throughout the summer, morel season was best in late spring.

In that first week of June I decided to take off on a Saturday, driving to a trailhead along the Leelanau Trail and then biking into Traverse City for some barhopping fun. Life in Glen Arbor could be spectacular and I'd experienced some incredible sunsets along the beaches in the park, but eventually I yearned for some nightlife involving others in my age bracket.

I arrived in the late afternoon and made my initial stop at a place called Workshop Brewing in what was referred to as the Warehouse District, although in reality it was just a street. The place was buzzing with drunken revelers who were part of a kayak, bike and brew tour. They'd crossed the Boardman Lake and then meandered down the Boardman River and the lakefront path, taking in more beer at various locations than would be advisable. Every one of them seemed happy and smashed in ill-fitting swimwear. I ordered a beer at the counter and took it out to the patio seating. It was a pleasant afternoon and I sat there watching the tourists and drunks—wondering when I would become one of them. Across the street a hotel was busy with bridal parties. Yes, they were cheesy but I was watching them like a spectator at a comedy club. Girls on a mission to get drunk could be so very entertaining. Compared to Glen Arbor this may as well have been SoHo in New York City.

There was activity with a sense of chaos not to be found for miles around in any direction. Small towns roll up there sidewalks early but Traverse City at least had a few pockets not conforming to that slumber.

I could have sat outside Workshop Brew for longer but I wanted to check out a place called Sleder's. Hannah had specifically mentioned the bear wearing a top hat in the front parlor window. I couldn't picture it. A bear in a top hat? She assured me it wasn't one of us. It was just a stuffed bear. Nonetheless, it was the sort of thing one of our clan would cringe at.

I biked along Randolph Street and locked up across from Sleder's next to an ice cream stand called the Dairy Lodge. A woman in a Santa Claus outfit was riding a huge ice cream cone on the rooftop. Not an actual woman, but that was their sign. "Ride that cone!" Was all I could think. So very strange, yet popular. The line at the window was at least six customers deep.

Crossing the street, the facade of Sleder's gave me pause. It looked similar to The Wooden Nickel where I'd met Blue. And sure enough, there was a small black bear in the front window with a dusty old top hat. I entered past the old popcorn machine and took a seat at one of the wooden booths beneath a montage of taxidermy. At least the interior was completely different from that bar in Marquette. A huge bison head hung alongside minks, raccoons, and the ever-necessary jackalope. But the star of the show was Randolph the moose. His gigantic head dominated the wall above the entrance to a back room parlor that used to be for women and Indians. Yes, this bar was that old. Apparently it stayed open even throughout prohibition. Patrons of the bar would still kiss— smooch—the moose and the bartender would ring insanely loud bells behind the bar to celebrate the occasion.

When I mention that, it almost makes the idea of having a connection with a spirit animal seem normal. Which it is.

The waitress came over in her 'I Smooched the Moose' t-shirt to take my order. I asked for a burger and of course, a Moosehead

beer, served up in a tallboy mug with a short handle. I sat back
to take in the colorful surroundings and watched a Tigers game
playing on the lone TV above the doorway to the kitchen. The place
was busy with a summer, early dinner crowd. Tourist families were
scattered throughout the tables with kids of all ages munching on
fries, urging their parents to kiss the moose so they could hear the
bells. Locals sat a the short, old fashioned bar with the brass foot
rail and vintage cash machine, talking to each other and receiving
town news from the bartender.

Across from me in the next booth over sat three men in what
sounded like a business meeting. The one facing me was an older
gentleman with a mustache, wearing a cowboy hat with the outline
of a tyrannosaur. I figured it to be some kind of expansion sports
team. He clearly was the one in charge. The other two middle-aged
men had their backs to me. I kept my eye on the baseball game
but my ear was eavesdropping their conversation, a habit I had
wherever I went. I always viewed it as free entertainment.

Cowboy Hat was talking while finishing off his sandwich. "We
were making progress with our offers until that local yokel woman
started alerting the residents to our concentrated efforts. It was
typical divide and conquer."

"Well, you won't need to worry about her anymore," added one
of the others. "We made it look like an accident."

"Boys, you might not want to be so brazen with your
declarations," noted Cowboy Hat. In my peripheral observation I
could see his hat scanning the crowd of loud, indifferent customers
happily enjoying their meals. Well, maybe not the table with the
fussy, crying child.

My waitress returned with my burger and beer, setting them
down in front of me. The burger looked unspectacular but
homemade and simple. Exactly what you'd expect and want. "Can
I get you anything else?" she asked in a pleasant voice that was also
busy with juggling more pressing requests. "No thanks," I answered,
"I'm good." And returned to listening in.

"No need for extreme caution," one of them was saying. "The remote switch for executing the steering would be destroyed in the crash and we gunked-up the seatbelt with common material like lint. It was just meant to take her out of commission for a while. The alternative result was an added benefit."

That's an odd car they're talking about, I was thinking. Sounds like one being prepped for some kind of smash-up derby. I was focused now on my food and tuned them out just as Cowboy Hat was getting up to leave, tossing dollars on the table.

I kept my foray into Sleder's brief and decided to hop over to another standard pub I'd heard about, Mackinaw Brewing Company. I rode along the lakefront trail taking in the scenic views of the West Bay, the beaches, and the volleyball courts still busy with bodies. I locked up my bike along the Boardman River at Cass Street and walked into another bustling scene coming off the evening rush. Fortunately there were a few seats at the long bar with spectators casually watching random sporting events playing across the TV screens over the line of tap handles. They were a friendly, mixed bunch and welcomed a single newcomer like myself with a nod to take one of the bar stools. I ordered up a pint of Red Ale and watched with mixed feelings as a plate of fried perch went by. My burger at Sleder's was good but that fish looked exceptional.

The pints were huge, imperial pints as they're referred to. Twenty ounce pours, not the standard sixteen. It didn't take long for conversations to open up with my fellow drinkers. On my left was an odd duck who apparently was an extreme regular capable of appearing normal despite consuming beer after beer after beer. His name was Bob and his conversation skills were about as lengthy as his name. After a few awkward attempts at communication I left him to the bartender and turned my attention to the group on my right. Now, these people were here to have a good time. The younger brunette girl in the group was drinking what appeared to be rum and coke, while the guy and the other girl were happy pounding drafts, full of smiles, side conversation antics, and actively watching the Tigers game who were tied in the 7th inning with the Royals.

"Our bullpen won't be able to pull this off," mentioned the guy, like a commentator for anyone within earshot.

I took that as an opportunity to join in. "Fortunately they're up against the lowly Royals." I wasn't sure about the standings in the AL Central but historically that was a good guess. Having been a Twins fan growing up I knew a thing or two about the Division even though I hadn't followed baseball closely since I was a kid.

As if on cue the Tiger's closer got the batter to chase a low slider, grounding it straight to the shortstop for a quick 6-4-3 double play. One pitch, inning over. A smattering of other patrons were clapping.

"You're a foreseer of good fortune," said the guy. "Are you a Tigers fan?"

"Actually a Twins fan. I grew up in Minneapolis. But I'm a baseball fan in general." Which was sort of true.

"Well, Twinkies fans are welcomed here, too. We're from downstate around the Detroit area but we love coming up here whenever we can." He was a big guy with a friendly disposition. One of those large presence people who no one bothers because of their size and consequently they're always open and central to any gathering.

"I'm Winnebago by the way. Like the RV. It's short for Winston, but nobody calls me that," he followed, jokingly. "Over here is Jackie."

The older of the two women leaned in with a "Hello." She was wearing really cool designer glasses that undoubtedly were from some European company.

"And that's Jenny." The younger one lifted her glass in greeting.

"Hey, there. What's your name?" she asked with a bubbly voice.

"Max." I answered.

Just then another couple took the last two seats at the end of the bar. The bartender, an older fellow who looked like he participated in triathlons, started putting out small pours of beer—in Wisconsin they'd call them sidecars or schnitts—he placed them in front of everyone at the bar, including himself. "Full bar salute!" He belted out. And everyone took a drink from the little glasses, some like Winnebago downing the contents entirely.

The game played on into extra innings and the social lubricants kept coming and going along with other people. A full bar salute would ebb and flow with the shifting seating. At least three of those happened alongside our standard orders. Clearly the bartender was in a good mood. The place had a lively feeling. The photos of cargo freighters, like the infamous Edmond Fitzgerald, lining the brick walls gave the place an industrial, maritime ambience. It felt more like an exclusive club than a brewpub. I was enjoying myself thoroughly.

The Tiger's bullpen held up well but their offense was non-existent and the Royals stole the game in the 11th, literally, with a single driving in a walked batter who previously made it to second on a wild pitch. "Damnit!" exclaimed Winnebago in the closing moment. "Oh, well. You lose some and you lose some. We should go out dancing someplace. I need a fun atmosphere after that."

From what I could tell, wherever this group went would be the fun atmosphere. They were a mobile party. And with that suggestion Jenny blurted out, "We could go to Side Traxx!"

"Yeah, that could be fun," responded Jackie. "We haven't been there before. Isn't that the gay bar? I think it's a bit of a walk, though."

"No worries. I can drive us," countered Jenny, giving legs to the idea. And so we settled up our tab and stepped out into the warm night. It was late but only just getting dark. Jenny's car was parked around back by my bicycle but we all piled into her small Toyota Camry, myself and Jackie taking the back allowing Winnebago the legroom afforded by the front passenger seat. Jenny's car was older and had that 'my first car' kind of vibe with a faded interior, discarded items on the floorboard, stuff dangling from the mirror, the tank under half-full, and a broken radio knob replaced with a cap from something else.

We wheeled out of the parking lot and drove what would have been a very walkable distance to Side Traxx, a single-story bar located at the end of a street along some old rail lines by the public library. There were a few guys standing outside on the patio, not wearing shirts, and smoking cigarettes. Jenny parked and we ambled across the empty street to the entrance, where the bouncer and a thumping bass-line greeted us. "$2 cover tonight." He didn't even bother checking IDs and instead kept his eye on the group on the patio. Jackie handed him a $10 to cover us all. Her look was sleek and stylish and she was a stark contrast to Winnebago who towered over our group in a Michigan State t-shirt, cargo shorts and Birkenstocks.

Inside, our motley quartet blended right into the dimly lit scene of colorful characters. It wasn't a huge place by any measure and felt like more like an office decorated for a dance party. Christmas lights were strung about everywhere and quirky posters, rainbow flags, and colorful messages hung upon the walls. A small disco ball and black lights illuminated the Mad Hatter checkerboard dance floor in the back where about 20 people could fit comfortably right next to the DJ. Guys in drag were playing darts, a bachelorette party with the bride-to-be was squawking and doing shots, and people of all types seemed to be having a groovy time.

We all headed straight to the bar like horses to the trough after a long ride through the desert. "What'll you have?" Winnebago called out above the music. Our replies didn't matter. He got us all a round of Coronas. I grabbed mine and wandered over toward the dance floor. The bridal party was out there and hey—I was young and single—and I started to move amongst the bodies. The DJ was mixing tracks of '80s tunes and *Like A Virgin* by Michigan's very own, Madonna, was playing to the audience. My numbers were favorable and I was a target of attention. I was grinding along when the track switched over to *Closer* by Nine Inch Nails. At that point the demographics of the dance floor shifted a little and I found myself 'closer' to guys and less of the bridal party, some who left but the ones remaining clearly had a connection with the lyrics.

"The bride and groom should walk down the aisle to this song!" someone loudly spoke into my ear. I looked over and saw Jenny dancing next to me. I welcomed her presence so I didn't give off the wrong vibe to the guys on the floor. My laissez-faire attitude toward life tended to invite unwanted advances.

I continued to dance with Jenny. "So, how do you know Winnebago and Jackie?" I asked. I hadn't really spoken much to her all night long since at Mackinaw Brew she was three bar stools over.

"I don't know them. I only met them tonight. Aren't they you're friends?" she replied.

That was unexpected. I inquired, "I thought they were your friends? You drove over here with them."

"No," she said, "I've never met them before. I'm not really supposed to be here, either. I'm only 18."

In my head a needle scratched across a record. ————————— What, no, what???

Thankfully the playlist had changed to the Go-Go's but suddenly I was overwhelmed with a sense of confusion. This was Winnebago and Jackie's friend, right? They were all at Mackinaw Brew, tourists from the Detroit area. Evidently, no. Way off. Where in the hell were Jackie and Winnebago anyway? I scanned the room, easily spotting Winnebago in the distance with Jackie, talking to a new group of people at the front of the bar.

"So, have you ever been here before? Weren't you drinking rum and cokes at Mackinaw Brew?" I was making conversation but my instinct to flee was setting in.

"No!" Jenny laughed, "those were just sodas. God, I would be wasted if that were the case. Sure, the bar salutes were fun but I was totally fine to drive over here if that's what you're worried about."

She happily continued to bounce around but I was starting to feel uncomfortable. The DJ began playing a dance version of *Sweet Dreams* by the Eurythmics and some guy started swaying up against me.

I tapped Jenny on the shoulder and leaned in to her ear, "Hey, I could use a refill. I'll be right back."

I won't lie; it felt murky leaving her on the dance floor. That girl had moxie and had been a convincing imposter throughout the night, but there was no good outcome to staying around any longer. She'll be fine, I figured. This was her wild adventure and she knew how to navigate it. I slipped through the crowd and out the front exit. The patio crowd had gotten larger and more boisterous. Scantily clad guys and girls were openly carousing in the unusually warm night. I crossed the road, got my bearings, and headed back into town walking through the dark, tree-lined neighborhoods. What an offbeat evening, I was thinking as I made my way down Washington Street. I'd never anticipate a place like Side Traxx in small town Michigan U.S.A.

When I finally got on my bike I was grateful to have my lights. It was going to be a challenging ride back to the Westie parked miles away at the trailhead. I hadn't intended on staying out *that* late. It was eerily quiet along the parkway path and I felt like a phantom gliding along. The bay looked calm and inviting and I decided to take a late night swim under the stars to clear my head. Their wasn't a soul on the beach at this hour so I left my bike and belongings next to some small trees and bushes providing cover just in case someone happened to come along. I walked into the water with only my boxers on. Usually I'd be squeamish with the cold but I dove into the shallow inky blackness and emerged on my back, looking up at the stars. Without the surrounding lights of downtown they were clear and countless.

The swim felt great, tranquil, *meditative*. And that's when the doors of perception *opened*.

I rolled, stretched out my arms and got in touch with my spirit animal at last.

The sensation was incredible and exhilarating, here I was, swimming as a bear under the stars. I hadn't even noticed that my boxers, also suspended in the water, ended up getting stretched to shreds. I felt slightly larger, but not huge, paddling around along the surface. I *had* been like this before with Blue. I could sense it with greater clarity.

But I kept it short. A bear swimming in the bay would probably be front page news should someone spot me circling about. I ducked underwater, transformed back into my human self, and started swimming to shore. Just like that, it was as easy as snapping your fingers. I couldn't wait to tell Hannah that we now shared a similar first time experience. She was positively going to be more ecstatic than me.

I climbed up the beach and quickly got dressed, feeling way more energized than expected. I was floating on cloud nine and barely registered the ride through the darkness of rolling birch stands and quiet fields. When I reached the Westie I thought it would be wise not to risk any further excitement. I was buzzing and I couldn't tell if it was the beers or the success of coming out of hibernation. Either way, I locked the bike to the rack and decided to sleep in the van. At first I couldn't stop my mind from racing but eventually I settled in and didn't wake up until the early morning sunrise glowed across the peninsula.

7

THE REAL LEGEND OF THE SLEEPING BEARS

The next morning I rolled into Hannah's driveway looking like something I might have run over. She was working in the studio and came out to greet me, with her faded jeans, t-shirt and hands all coated with clay. She was a splendid sight even when messy.

I floundered out of the Westie and greeted her with a feigned smile, knowing what I must have looked like. "Wouldn't happen to be cooking up a late breakfast, would you?" I jested, knowing full well from her appearance that she was working the potter's wheel. I hadn't eaten since Sleder's and was starving. She could tell I was feeling a little rough around the edges.

"Well, well, well, Maximilian. Looks like you had quite the night." Hannah was strolling up the driveway, wiping off her hands on a towel. She had a twinkle in her eyes and an ever-widening grin across her face. "You seem different, kid. Meet a new girl or something?"

So far in our relation, Hannah hadn't seen me return from an extended night out. The nightlife scene in The County simply did not warrant revelry well past midnight. I felt like I was returning home to a college roommate who was going to needle me with commentary for the rest of the day.

"Oh, better than that," I answered matter-of-factly.

She raised her hands, "I don't need to hear all the details like that, Max. TMI. The saying is a gentleman never tells."

It took me a moment to see what she was implying. "No. *Better than that*," I emphasized and stood there watching her face.

Hannah stopped and tilted her head, her eyes widening with inquiry, "Did you…?"

"Yep. No more hibernating for this member of the Sleeping Bear Clan." I think I may have done that silly double thumb-pointing motion at myself.

Next thing I knew she was giving me a huge bear hug, lifting my feet off the ground, kissing me on the cheek. "I'm elated for you, Max! Finally the meditation practice pays off."

She squeezed me again before setting me down, "Oh, this calls for a celebration and I can tell you're hungry. I've got some awesome bread and leftover bluegill from last night's dinner with Bern. Sorry about the clay on your clothes. Let's head inside and I'll fix up something. I want to hear all about it."

We walked in through the studio; the industrial sliding door was wide open to the living quarters of her house. The radio was picking up some Sunday morning blues program out of WNMC, the local collage station. Hannah walked straight to her retro Smeg refrigerator and pulled out a bottle of Sex, a local pink bubbly made my Mawby Vineyards on the other side of Lake Leelanau.

"First, some hair of the dog," announced Hannah. "Apologies if you're not feeling it quite yet, but I've had this stored in the refrigerator just for this occasion." She poured the champagne into glasses you might typically use for juice or a short cocktail. Hannah wasn't one to have a bunch of high-end stemware.

She slid mine over across the counter and lifted her own.

"Cheers, and here's to being awake!" We clinked glasses and we each took a big swig. I was grateful for having such a cool mentor.

"So, where'd it take place? How'd it happen?" she quizzed.

"You won't believe it. It was just like you. I was swimming in the West Bay." My answer surprised her.

"Get out!" she interjected. "Wait. That's a pretty public location. Were there people around, did anyone see you?" she added with a hint of concern.

"No, it was after midnight, there was no one around, and it was super dark. The air was so warm and calm that I decided to take a swim on my way back from a rather unusual time in TC. The water was refreshing and while I was floating around looking up at the stars it just—clicked." Saying it out loud was reassuring to myself that it actually did happen.

"I know exactly what you mean," she beamed. "And I'm glad it wasn't daylight. Although people might not believe their eyes anyway. Incidents like that have happened before, though." Hannah finished her drink and poured us each another, "That's tasting pretty good."

She continued, "Anyhow, if you search the local news archives, you can find occasional reports of bears running through town. And while usually it is only a bear, other times it's one of our fellow clan members who got super drunk and then forgot our unspoken rules of not running about in public. I can think of one episode not too long ago where the *Record-Eagle* carried a front page photo of a bear running down an alley in the old warehouse district and our folks in The County were like, 'That's Zoey. What was she thinking?'"

We had our impromptu brunch of cold fish on warm buttered toast and Michigan champagne while I filled in the details about my excursion into town. Hannah was particularly amused with the spectacle at Side Traxx. "Winnebago and Jackie sound like quite the partying odd couple. And I cannot believe that Jenny!" she said. "That girl has balls."

As we finished up I could feel my balance returning. When Hannah suggested hiking the Alligator Trail I was all for it. As with anywhere, weekdays were best for expeditions to the public parks but Sunday afternoons were usually less crowded, too, as weekenders returned to their homes elsewhere.

"Get yourself set to roll," Hannah directed. "I'll round up some trail mix. We can ride our bikes to the trailhead."

Compared to last night's trek in the dark, the ride out to the trailhead was a breeze. We followed backroads and part of the Heritage Trail before swinging south along Stocking Road. Surprisingly the small parking lot was empty, which was a sign that we would likely have the trail to ourselves. We locked up the bikes and started up the short incline.

"We'll walk to the Glen Lake overlook and loop back. It's a great little hike. And the overlook of the Manitous is beautiful," Hannah sounded like a park ranger.

The path was sandy and wide, with the springtime foliage changing over to summer. A small garter snake slithered across the trail in front of us. We paused to watch him slide off into the brush.

"The Manitous. Those are the two islands representing the bear cubs in the Sleeping Bear legend, right? The ones that didn't make it," I asked, making small talk.

Hannah turned to take in the surrounding scenery. "Not exactly," she answered, "that's the local yarn and accepted version for kids books. Although that story is rooted in reality. The real Legend of the Sleeping Bears is more tragic."

"How so?" I couldn't imagine something more depressing than the story of a mother bear and two cubs swimming across Lake

Michigan only to have the two cubs drown, thus forming North and South Manitou Islands, while the mother waited for them in vain and eventually turned into the huge dunes the park was famously known for.

"It's the story of our clan," she remarked as we continued along a gradual incline through the woods. "It goes way back, to the First Peoples."

"What do you mean First Peoples? Like out of Africa evolutionary paths? Or maybe some kind of exodus out of the spirit world?" They both seemed a stretch. But then, a lot of what I though I knew was being tossed aside.

"Sort of but not quite that extensive. More like the first people on this side of the world," Hannah clarified.

"The short version goes like this. About 25,000 years ago before the end of the last ice age, a group of humans inhabited land called Beringia between what is now Alaska and Russia, and is currently under the Bering Sea. You can genetically trace almost all of the pre-Columbian people on this side of the world to that group. Sure, perhaps there have been others. Nordic people via Greenland. Polynesians being thrown off course, somehow crossing the vast Pacific. Chinese sailing expeditions. Fine. Theories and long forgotten integrations. But who's certain to say. 25,000 years is a long time in human history. Think about it. The pyramids were only 3,000 years ago. Rome only 2,000 years. Europeans 'discovering' the New World only about 500 years."

I loved when Hannah really got into telling a story. She could be enthralling.

We were getting to a point along the trail where many of the trees appeared missing, snapped in half or fallen. "I want to hear the rest of that story, but what happened here?" I asked.

"Huge storm a few years ago came in off Lake Michigan and just leveled the area here and in other parts around the region. This path used to be completely shaded, now it's more like walking through an open meadow. Logs like those older growth trees over there," she was pointing to some giant fallen timbers, "could fetch a lot of money if they were harvested. But since this is a national park they're left alone, much to the chagrin of some lumber companies. Give it twenty years and it will all come back."

"But back to the story and history of our clan," I didn't want her to get off track.

"Right. Where was I? Oh, yeah. The people living in the Bering Straits 25,000 years ago," she recalled. "They were what we refer to as the First Peoples. And somewhere, somehow in that place and time they connected with the spirit world. Remember when I mentioned there being other clans with different spirit animals? Well, they also derive from this group. And when the Ice Age ended and the glaciers retreated, they spread out across the Americas setting up civilizations great and small, rise and fall, deep into the Amazon and jungles, along the coasts, into the valleys and high into the mountains.

"So, that's the beginning of our unique genetic capability—being able to transform into bears—and it's why I'm uncertain if there are other clans with spirit animals in other parts of the world like Europe, Asia, Africa, Australia. We know our place here, but I'm not aware of clans on those other continents. Maybe at that time the connection with the spirit world happened all over and to other people. Maybe that's the start of religion, mythology, gods and legends."

We'd reached a fork along the trail and Hannah paused. "Let's check out this overlook now. It ties in well with the story."

We followed a short spur off the main loop to a spectacular view overlooking the Manitou Straits. In the distance to the right was North Manitou Island. Slightly closer was South Manitou Island. And to our left along the coastline were the Sleeping Bear Dunes. The water was a magnificent green-aqua-blue.

"Anyhow, our particular clan started out there in Alaska and gradually moved east onto the plains. You have to remember, these Great Lakes didn't even exist back then. They were under ice."

Hannah motioned with her hand indicating the view. It was difficult to imagine this huge body of water not existing.

"Eventually about 5,000 B.C. the lake outlines as we know them came into being. And it was sometime, millennia later that our clan was in conflict with other Plains peoples. Oral histories speak of battles with other clans. I cannot imagine what those would have been like. No horses, of course. Those were introduced by Europeans thousands of years later. So it would have been chaotic skirmishes with clubs, arrows, spears and probably warriors transforming into their spirit animal whenever that proved advantageous. Being a bear can be powerful but you also can't pick up a weapon, and you become a much larger target. Or something like changing into a raven could give you an immediate retreat."

She glanced over to see how I was taking it all in. "Sorry, I'm rambling down a tangent."

"And so that's where these islands and dunes in the distance before you fit into the picture. It wasn't bear cubs that were lost. Rather it was two groups from our clan. The histories say we lost the battles and were pursued relentlessly by a confederation of other clans and people in an attempt to wipe us out. Why, is unclear.

"Our clan was surrounded near what is now the Door County peninsula in Wisconsin. In a desperate effort to escape, they attempted to cross Lake Michigan in three great armadas of canoes. The first tribe landed safely where the dunes are, but the other two were lost to a terrible storm, probably similar in ferocity to the one that tore the tops off all these trees."

"Wait a minute," I was trying to envision this happening. "You've covered an extremely long stretch of time, from people living alongside mammoths to late pre-Columbian America. How many people are we talking about? And how is it you have such a fair complexion? Why don't you look more Native American?"

This real Legend of the Sleeping Bears was too fantastical and wasn't adding up.

"The genetics exist. Maybe they always have. It doesn't require a dominant trait to continue on. As for me, a lot of European settlers to this region happened to be from Germany, Scandinavia, Northern Europe. A few generations later this is what you end up with," she moved her hands like she was scanning herself.

"Think of you, living in Minnesota, in hibernation," Hannah said, using my history as an example. "Your family had no idea this world—being connected with a spirit animal—ever existed. Yet the ability gets passed on in some of the most improbable manners. And you, Max, are likely related to a remnant tribe that escaped along a different route. Or maybe your roots trace back to a lost canoe in that fateful storm."

"But my parent's histories are from Sweden and Norway," I countered. "They wouldn't be part of that First Peoples group you're talking about."

"Well, I hate to break it to you, kid, but somewhere along the line one of your relatives got it on with someone native," she playfully admonished. "How about some of that trail mix?"

I retrieved the snack from my backpack, thinking about my family background and how little I really knew about it. "Could it be that everyone in the world has a spirit animal connection but only .00001% of us are not hibernating?"

"That could be, Max. But in your case Blue tagged you as one of us. She's not the type to make an errant assessment. Come on, let's continue to the Glen Lake Overlook."

We headed back to the main trail and hiked the short distance to a stand of huge pines overlooking Glen Lake. These trees had survived the storm of the century. The surroundings and pine-needle-covered grounds were a stark contrast to the fallen logs and broken branches only a quarter of a mile back. It felt quiet.

"So, how long has our clan been living here in The County?" I asked, seeking a more definitive time-line.

"The surviving clan members decided to make this region their new home and have been here ever since, living among the various Anishinaabe like the Odawa and Ojibwa, the French explorers, the colonists, the British, the Americans and now everyone. I know. It's hard to believe," she said.

Hannah anticipated my next question, "And no, it's not like everyone stays here or are from Michigan. Members of our community move on elsewhere for jobs, warmer climates, and better opportunities just like everybody else. But the common thread is most of our clan members have a connection to the people or this area in some fashion."

"So why not establish communities elsewhere?" I asked. It seemed sensible.

"Oh, it's been done or tried but this has been our home base, so to speak, for ages, where we can keep our practices and community awake. As human populations have grown around urban centers, the connection with nature and the spirit world gets lost, replaced by industry and technologies. A community like ours in a city? That would be like practicing meditation in a mosh pit at a punk rock concert. It just isn't going to work." Hannah used interesting analogies at times.

"You say it's been tried. Where about? Like, are we affiliated with the professional football team in Chicago?" I asked, half-joking.

"They haven't been much of a team since the mid-80's. I'm not sure we'd want to be affiliated with them," Hannah answered wryly. "Funny observation, but no. I've never even thought about it. People pick mascots for a variety of reasons."

She continued, "However, one of our clan's more colorful dramas involved a fellow named James Strang. He wasn't one of us, but he and his Mormon followers basically took over Beaver Island in the mid-1800s. He declared himself King of the Island! That didn't go over well with our clan members settled there. He pretty much pushed around anyone who didn't adhere to his religious tenants. Eventually Strang was shot and killed and afterwards clan members from around the area descended on the island and drove out his remaining congregation, retaking the land. But relations to our community are far more spread out now then they were back then. Travel is simply much easier."

We started heading back along the trail. I was thinking how the spirit world connection in the past was probably much more beneficial than today.

"Hannah, how is it you know all this stuff?" I questioned. "Don't tell me you're secretly 2,000 years old."

"Geez, Max. Don't you know? Don't ever ask a girl's age," she knocked my upper arm with a false punch. "I'm only 45 years young. As for knowing our history, it's part of who we are. My parents told me the stories just like I'm telling you. We also have a historical society and community librarian. They're like the crazy relatives who keep track of family trees. And of course there are spirit bears like Blue with a more direct connection."

"What about the folks in Peshawbestown?" I was referring to the Grand Traverse Band of Ottawa and Chippewa Indians who operated a casino north of Suttons Bay.

"Oh yeah, we have loads of community members with them. Remember, even when our one tribe successfully crossed Lake Michigan there were plenty of people already living here. They've definitely been in the mix for a long, long while, and have been instrumental in maintaining the environment in The County for years and years. But don't think that they're all part of our clan. They have their own culture and traditions and are now a mixed bag of everyone and different groups as well."

Far up the path, we could see a man and woman with a dog walking in our direction so Hannah wrapped up her story quickly.

"Unfortunately for the Grand Traverse Band and everyone else on this side of the world, when the Europeans arrived, the disease they brought with them was apocalyptic. Entire communities wiped out within a generation. Imagine how dysfunctional things would be if ninety percent of your community members died.

"At times I find it astounding that anyone with our ability survived. It surprises me that other, equally disastrous pathologies haven't happened," Hannah continued.

"I always compare it to the story of the American Chestnut, a gigantic tree that blanketed eastern North America. Thoreau's famous Walden Woods were full with them. Yet, in the late 1800's a fungus blight from Asia ended up killing an estimated 4 billion trees—that's billion with a B—making them technically extinct, all within the incredibly short time frame of a single generation. A child would have no concept of the majestic trees their grandparents knew as being everywhere. Most people today are completely unaware of that story, just as they are with a lot of history."

I have to admit, I'd never heard about the American Chestnut, either.

We crossed paths with the couple and their dog, a happy black lab who accepted our attention with great enthusiasm. The afternoon was getting warmer and I was grateful we had been able to share such an open discussion without the interruption of others.

We biked back into Glen Arbor and Hannah suggested picking up sandwiches from Anderson's Market. At the checkout counter there was a bookrack selling local publications for tourists. One of them was a children's book titled *The Legend of Sleeping Bear*.

I tossed it on the checkout conveyor with our sandwiches. Hannah just gave me a look that said, "Really?"

A Sinister Truth Revealed

Later that week Bern stopped over for the night. Hannah invited me to have dinner with them. She was always inclusive like that, although I had figured out when to politely leave the house to them. A Motown playlist emanated from the speakers. The Temptations were playing. You could sense these two were extremely happy when they were together and the music only enhanced that.

We were gathered around the table with talk about how successful this year's season was compared to the previous year. By season, I'm referring to the Tourist Season, conventionally marked from Memorial Day to Labor Day. Which, if mentioned to any local, invariably gets the old joke response, "Why call it Tourist Season if you can't shoot them?" So far, this year had been average, at least for Hannah's gallery. But she hadn't had a mortgage payment in years, owned her home and studio outright, so an average year of sales was plentiful.

Working in her shop throughout the week, I got a good feel for the flow of business in the Glen Arbor area. Tourists and the cottagers tended to bustle about late morning to early evening, but most returned to their summer homes, resorts and BnBs for the night or headed to the beach to catch the sunset. Nightlife in The County deferred primarily to Traverse City or the casino in

Peshawbestown, although Frankfort and Manistee occasionally had something going, too.

I hadn't seen Bern since revealing to Hannah the end of my hibernation. He was enjoying a mead and when Hannah got up to check on some noodles cooking on the stove he looked over at me. "Max, I haven't been able to place it, but since I walked in that door you seem—different." He then asked to both Hannah and me, "Am I right?"

"You're on to something, Bern," Hannah said from the stove, back turned towards us. "I've been curious myself."

I paused. These two had their own language, as couples do over time. I couldn't always decipher it but you could sense when they were talking to each other with the slightest of signals and voice inflections. I picked up on where Hannah was steering the conversation.

"You're right, Bern. I'm awake. No longer hibernating," my delivery was deadpan.

"Is that so!" Bern exclaimed. "Well, congratulations, Max. How did it happen? What do you look like?"

I answered his first question with an overview of my late night swim in the Grand Traverse West Bay, just like I told Hannah. Bern chuckled at the similarities between the stories, both hers and mine. "I cannot believe you two, transcending with your spirit animal for the first time while swimming. What are the odds? I don't know of anyone else in our clan to experience that," he was shaking his head.

"I know. I thought it was a surreal coincidence," I answered and left it at that.

Hannah took the pasta off the stove top, pouring it into a colander while saving a couple cups of the water. "Max, I've been wondering as well. What do you look like? We've not seen you in your spirit animal, yet."

I had been shy about sharing my self-discovery even with fellow clan members as intimate as Hannah and Bern, who had become very much like surrogate parents. Although I had practiced transforming ever since coming out of hibernation, I did it alone, in Hannah's studio, or at night just outside the Westie in the obscurity and seclusion of the backyard. Obviously, there was a fascination about it, like a kid learning to ride a bicycle, a teenager learning to drive. You wanted to perfect it as mindlessly as tying your shoes.

"Let's have a pre-dinner show," Bern stated like a spectator at a staged play. "Change in the studio and make a grand entrance."

I wasn't going to argue. It was going to happen sooner or later, so why not make it now. I got up and walked past the large sliding door and into the studio. The lights were off and curtains were drawn, so I wasn't concerned with the long shot of someone seeing me from the roadway. I ditched my clothing and slipped into my bear form and re-entered the main house to the sound of applause.

"Look at you!" I could hear Hannah saying, "He's got some lighter coloring and a slightly crooked ear."

Bern continued clapping, "Well done, Max. Bravo. We'll be able to easily identify you now." In a manner, I stood up on my back legs and attempted a bow before sauntering off to the studio to transform back to my human self. I felt like I was modeling this year's fashion. I considered what that would have looked like to an outsider. Two adults preparing dinner when a bear walks into the room and all they do is laugh and applaud.

"How was that?" I called out to the kitchen.

"Excellent," was the reply from Bern. "You'll have to showcase that at The Bear Lunar."

"What's that?" I had no idea what he was talking about.

"Get on in here and have some puttanesca and we'll tell you all about it," Hannah was saying.

They filled in some general details about a festival that members of our clan held every other year out on the Manitou Islands. Some people gathered on the North Island but generally the South Island was preferred because of its more manageable size. Others held events inland and elsewhere throughout the region, even on Beaver Island and the North and South Fox Islands. Members sought remote locations where they could gather as bears and consume barrels of intoxicating meads. Within the clan some used its Ojibwa name Makwa Oshkagoojin (Bear New Moon) since it coincided with the first full moon in August. But in general it was known as The Bear Lunar.

The every-other-year aspect was in reverence of the balance between the material and spirit worlds. It was a celebration of the continuation of the clan, a remembrance of the lost tribes, an affirmation of a commitment to the environment, and an opportunity to socialize in an unconventional manner.

"There's nothing quite like it," Bern said, stating the obvious. "Hannah and I prefer the gathering on South Manitou when we can make it. We'll bring you along now that you're no longer hibernating. You won't want to miss it."

I could—and could not—imagine it. And I was thankful to have such accommodating guides. And food. "This is delicious. What did you call it again?"

"Puttanesca," Hannah answered. "Bern made it for me early on when we were getting to know each other. It was one of his go-to recipes for first dates. Isn't that right?"

"Correct. It's super simple. Even I could make it. Pasta, garlic, tomatoes, capers, kalamata olives, and loads of fresh parsley. Its name is derived from the Italian word for whore," he was smiling intentionally at Hannah, "not that I'm implying anything."

She threw a wet dishtowel at him, connecting with his face. "Whatever, you jackass," she playfully responded.

I was getting that feeling like I might need to retire to the Westie or the studio in just a while.

"Well, regardless of that endearing narrative, it's been a great meal yet super energizing. I think I'll take an evening bike ride before it gets too dark." Evenings this time of year could stay light outside well past 10 P.M.

"That sounds like a good plan, Max," said Hannah, not suggesting that they would be joining me. "We'll probably meet up with you at the party for Kate in Leland tomorrow. I'm heading over to Bern's place in Suttons Bay tonight. We have to meet up with some other friends coordinating some logistics with that. So, when you get back from your ride feel free to use the whole house. We'll probably be out of here by then."

"Oh, thanks," I said and started to head out. They each got up and gave me a hug. I felt like I had a new family. "I'll see you tomorrow, then."

***

The following evening I started up the Westie in preparation to head to the party celebrating Kate's life. I tried to make a drive in the Westie at least once every week just to keep it running and operational. The event was being held on a private farm belonging to someone who wasn't a member of our clan. I was somewhat surprised by that, but Kate was definitely a well-respected member of all communities, not just our clan. It wasn't going to be a formal affair and that worked out well for my wardrobe.

When I arrived, the front lot of the estate had been converted into an open field parking lot. Cars were spread about, loosely organized in rows, all with the usual bumper stickers and accessories I'd become accustomed to seeing. TC, GL, SB, LA, LOVE with the state outline tilted in place of the 'V', UP, 26.2, 70.3, 0.0, Bell's Beer, Shorts Brewing, Hop Lot, this vineyard and that, Great Lakes outline, racks for bikes, kayaks, canoes, and the ever present M-22 sticker. You might get the feeling people here really enjoyed their local beverages and being active. And you'd be right.

The primary venue was an old, vintage barn converted into event space. Rustic, heavy wooden beams were complemented by creative lighting. There was no formal presentation or dinner but plenty of appetizers, food tables, local wines and beers. A bluegrass-inspired band thumped out background music and some dance tunes. Photo collages spread about the grounds indicated a life well lived. Kate had been a popular carpenter, contractor and active community member. Many of her clients and collaborators were in attendance. It had the feeling of a wedding crossed with a kegger. By now I could hold my own with the natives. I'd been working out of Hannah's studio for over a month and I recognized plenty of familiar faces in the crowd. I was making my way over to the bar when I bumped into Bern and Hannah chatting with some people I didn't know.

"Hey there! Good to see you made it. I'm never sure about that Westie of yours," Hannah was speaking above the noise of the crowd. Bern gave my shoulder a tap. "These are our friends, Will and Petra. They live in Suttons Bay and were helping us with some of the event preparation last night. Guys, this is Max. He's been working at Hannah's shop this summer."

I greeted them with a handshake. As Petra let go she pointed out my tattoo. "Ah, you're *that* boy. We've heard a bit about you. Nice to put a face to the name."

It was obvious that they were also members of our clan. They seemed to be the same vintage as Hannah and Bern, perhaps a few years older. Same healthy, slim builds, yet both of them with darker hair. "Hannah says you're quite a biking enthusiast," said Will. "Road bike, fat tire, trails. What type?"

"I've got a general road bike. Not too high-end but sleek enough for distance," I replied. "The trails in The County are awesome. It's also nice that a lot of the roads aren't heavily trafficked."

We got to talking about excursions, establishments to visit, my background and theirs. Turns out they were married with two daughters, one working on Capitol Hill in D.C. and the other starting her career in Lansing.

"We both grew up around here but met while working in Detroit," Will was saying. "Eastern Market was certainly different back then. From there it just clicked and we decided to return to the area when we wanted to start a family."

That was a common theme for a lot of residents—leaving to try out life elsewhere only to realize home was more special than a lot of other places.

Hannah got pulled away to somewhere else. Bern returned and handed me a bottled beer. "These two," Bern was indicating Will and Petra "have been good friends for years. Hannah and I used to hang out with them before they had Charlotte and Lea. We've had some times to say the least."

Will and Petra were fun to talk to and we continued until they spotted other guests they needed to connect with. I moved on to mingling with others, overhearing conversations about Kate, some expressing shock about the way she died in the accident, but mostly stories of a character who had charmed and touched the lives of a lot of people.

I was grazing at one of the food tables when Hannah came by with a backpack. "Max, I'll need to catch a ride with you when this event is over. Can you toss this in the Westie? I'm afraid I'll forget it later on."

"Sure, no problem," and I took the backpack while she was off again. I exited the barn and walked out to the rows of parked cars. The Westie was near the driveway entrance. When I parked, I didn't want to chance driving too far into the yard where the less-than-utility vehicle could get stuck in a rut. I noticed a pickup truck passing by that grabbed my attention. On its side was the outline of a Tyrannosaur with the words Texas Real Estate Exchange. It took a moment before I realized that it was the same logo I saw on the cowboy hat the man was wearing at Sleder's. The two men in the cab looked vaguely familiar like the guys who were sitting opposite of Cowboy Hat.

I felt a chill run down my spine, *and that's when the dots started connecting.*

Their conversation from that Saturday—I'd been hearing the consequence of it all afternoon: "Made it look like an accident. The remote switch for the steering. Meant to take her out." They had been talking about sabotaging Kate's car and her death was the "added benefit."

I stood there, stunned by the epiphany, watching them slowly cruising by then speeding up along the road. What were they doing here? I wondered. Returning to the scene of the crime. Making sure everything was calm. Surveying the community reaction.

I was going to have to tell Hannah and Bern. But perhaps not right now. I turned, heading back to the gathering when I realized I was still carrying Hannah's backpack. I doubled back to the Westie and tossed it on the floorboard while scanning the road, expecting to see another T-Rex drive-by.

The rest of the afternoon took on a surreal atmosphere with my newfound insight. The celebration suddenly felt like an inauspicious occasion. I wandered the crowd looking at the photo displays thinking, "Murdered. Why?"

As evening progressed people gradually dispersed. Hannah and I said goodbye to Bern who was riding back with Will and Petra. As we jumped into the Westie Hannah asked, "You okay to drive home? You seem a little quiet. That was a good crowd. I got to catch up with so many people." She looked relaxed.

I assured her I capped off my drinking hours ago, and we preceded the drive back to her home and studio. But I couldn't hold my thoughts any longer.

"Hannah, I've got to tell you something that's going to sound a bit unsettling. Particularly given the party we just attended."

Having no idea what to expect, her expression was indifferent. "I think Kate was murdered by the T-Rex company."

She quickly shifted to incredulous. "Whaaaat? No. She died in an accident, Max. We just have to accept it. What makes you think that she was intentionally killed?"

"That night I went into Traverse City, when I stopped at Sleder's like you suggested, I happened to be seated next to a group of guys having a peculiar exchange." It was coming back to me clearer and clearer. "The boss—if that's what you might call him—was wearing a cowboy hat with the T-Rex logo. Initially I thought it was some sort of sports team. Or maybe a local racing team. The two guys he was with were talking about disabling the steering on a vehicle, taking someone out. I didn't put it altogether until just this afternoon when I saw those same two men driving by in a T-Rex pickup truck, like they were checking out the party."

"What did the cowboy hat guy look like?" Hannah was more engaged, now.

"Tall. Mustache. Older. Graying hair." I wasn't overly elaborate.

"Sounds like the jerk who runs that company," her face had a cringe of disgust. "Liam Wallace. 'Liar' Wallace is favored by people who've done business with him. So, you're certain you saw the *same* guys driving past the party?"

"If it wasn't, then there's another set of T-Rex employees randomly riding around The County that look just like them." I was sure it was the same two men. "It adds up. They're surveying the scene to see how the community is reacting. Everyone is accepting Kate's death as an accident while they're getting away with murder. She was incredibly disruptive to their attempts at getting residents to sell out to their development plans and bribes. And now—like they put it—'she's out of the way'."

"She was also one of the county commissioners," Hannah was building the case in her own way. "Max, I need to look into this more but I think you might be on to something. There have been some incidents building dissent among residents and now those don't seem so innocent."

"Like what?"

"I've been hearing stories in town and at the studio. Neighbor blaming neighbor for this failure or that. Officials suddenly in favor of approving development measures." I could tell Hannah was making up her mind. "Something isn't right."

We were approaching her home at the close of a long day. I pulled into the driveway and swung the Westie to its usual spot along the side of the studio. Hannah was closing the passenger door, saying, "We can't let Kate's death slip through the cracks. If this is true the clan will want justice, so I don't want to alarm the community or start putting out accusations until I gather more information. I'm going to have to sleep on this—if I can. Geez, not the ending to the day I was expecting. I'll see you in the morning." And she walked off distractedly into the house.

That night my sleep was restless and I had a dream of trees, attempting to communicate with me, telling me to be vigilant.

9

FATHER OF THE BRIBE

Liam—'Liar'—Wallace had earned his reputation. He specialized in distorting facts, spinning stories and twisting statistics as a means to an end. He'd grown up an only child to a set of wealthy parents living off an inheritance of land, long ago taken away unjustly from someone else. He spent his youth being doted upon; getting anything he wanted, evermore building a sense of entitlement to everything. As a child he had a few friends but none very close. Dogs instinctively disliked him and he had a scar across his forearm from a black lab that bit him when he tried pushing the dog into a pool.

In grade school he was disruptive but never disciplined on account of his parents' standing in the community. Faculty members wanted to keep their jobs, not become embroiled with threats of lawsuits that their teacher salaries couldn't compete with. No, it was better to just give him a passing grade and send him along to the next unlucky soul. And so, little Liam learned at an early age that authority could easily be pushed aside with accusations, deceit, and money.

In high school he grew out of his short, pudgy frame and sprouted like a weed. His new height gave him an advantage over his classmates, lending an air of superiority and stature. He was a decent athlete and tried out for solo sports like tennis and golf.

Being part of a true team unit—like a baseball team or football squad—sharing the spotlight of importance, didn't appeal to his image. He considered himself to be self-made, albeit he never worked an honest day in his life. Of course, he had all the modern gadgets and clothing styles that affluence could buy. Where others might take a bus—my god, public transportation—Liam drove to school from twice as far, in a fraction of the time, in a shiny new convertible. And girls noticed. Why not date the fellow with connections, cash, transportation and impunity from the local police? Sounds like he could be much more fun and entertaining than some poor schlep actually working after school. And Liam knew how to take advantage of that.

Some of his earliest experiences dating involved hookers. Driving into the city, his car was a virtual advertisement saying, "Here's a paycheck and I'm not a fat old man." He appreciated the transactional aspect of it, getting what he wanted without the emotional investment or attachment of a relationship. These brokered rendezvous did not impart a dignified framework for dealing with the opposite sex. Liam's dates with fellow classmates were one-sided affairs often ending abruptly if she failed to comply with his sexual advances. Initially he would be charming, then calculating, then cunning, and often, forceful. His most successful romance lasted two weeks and officially ended a month later with an out-of-state visit to a clinic.

After high school, Liam attended a university and naturally joined a fraternity where his wealth could pave over his social deficiencies. There he was in his element, prowling the campus with a disingenuous band of brothers. They earned an abusive reputation that was forgotten by every new wave of freshmen girls. Their exploits were shared and exaggerated within the group and Liam at last found peers he could be brash and open with in expressing his views and values. For him, women were another commodity to capitalize. And that may as well have been his degree.

His formal education was merely a distraction. A right of passage. Following graduation Liam didn't have to search for employment, worry about paying back student loans, nor concern himself with car payments, insurance rates, or savings. He went to work for the real estate holdings company that his father established. He was a capable employee, albeit reckless at times with his investment decisions. Not that any of his poor dealings ultimately mattered. He was the golden boy. Heir to the throne. And when his father passed away he put his mother out to pasture in a retirement community and re-branded the company with a dinosaur logo. He had been fascinated by the prehistoric creatures throughout his life and admired the predatory image of the Tyrannosaurus rex.

To secure deals, his company leaned on buy-outs, intimidation and blackmail. When those failed, they excelled at exploiting animosities between vested interests. Texas Real Estate Exchange was successful always at the expense of others. After all, that was the game. That's what made it purposeful and fun. Mutually beneficial arrangements weren't to be expected. There were winners and losers. Nothing else mattered and collateral damage was an excepted norm. It was with that tactical approach that Liam and his team were operating in their endeavor to develop the lakeshore south of Leland.

There had been a few bumps in the road but Liam felt they were closing-in on getting the permits and contracts needed to establish the foundation for his planned resort village. They had been working the county commissioners, setting up meetings and expensed luncheons. This was the company's first foray into Michigan and they couldn't lean on state-level political connections and coercion to sway the decisions. Yet, in a way, working on the locals was easier and more direct. For a while a swing vote was needed. Now, with that pesky Kate woman out of the way, who also happened to be the 5th District Commissioner, a spot had opened up where T-Rex could be far more influential. It always amused Liam Wallace how a single vote could be all that was needed to alter the course of a development, and for that matter, the landscape of an entire township. How foolish people could be in not paying attention to the local politics that they had the most influence over. Obtaining that official backing was a challenge and great entertainment. He relished sealing the deal and then crushing the opposition once he got the upper hand.

And this time was no different. The T-Rex team secured some open-lots and farmland, but their initial attempts to buy-out residents with shoreline access proved unsuccessful. So, they started digging into backgrounds, tax records, archived news records and most importantly, gossip. They had discovered one plot of land with a home partially built over the location of a common area easement. How unfortunate for the owner to have that discovery brought up at the next county meeting. And it was important to keep the motivation behind such research anonymous. That way speculation and false truths could breed mistrust and unfounded grievances between the parties involved. Divide and conquer was a tried-and-true means to getting owners to give in to purchase offers T-Rex would extend.

For instance, a T-Rex agent discovered one of the lake-access homeowners had a couple dogs that preferred to use the neighbor's yard as a toilet. This irked the neighbor. To provoke a conflict, Liam directed the agent to take a bag of dog shit and toss it through an open window of the dog owner's car. Well, whom do you think the dog owner suspected of doing that? They knew where their dogs went.

Liam then personally followed-up, going a step further. In this case his disdain for dogs only heightened his malice. He tossed poisoned pieces of steaks into the yard when the dogs were out playing. The pair of friendly, approachable golden retrievers couldn't resist their good fortune and it cost them dearly, eventually dying later on that day. Not that Liam cared about the dogs. And of course the one neighbor would be incredulous, denying everything because in truth they did nothing. But that's not how things would be perceived. He now he had a full-on war between two lakefront properties and he certainly could get one, and then the other, to sell-out. Who wants to live next to an enemy? They could buy a dream house elsewhere and the T-Rex vision of *Lakeland Estates* could move forward.

Yes, things were moving along nicely. And it didn't stop with agitating the residents. There were tracts of land marked for preservation due to the old-growth trees standing on the property.

Typical tree-huggers obstructing progress, was how Liam saw that argument. His solution to circumvent that issue was simple: cut the trees down at night when no one was guarding them. Not himself, off course. But a team from out-of-state, hired through a third party. Some fake documentation, a promise of payment from a shell company, authentic-looking letterhead and business cards, and you could get a small team of bumpkins with chainsaws and pickup trucks to agree to just about anything. Was it expensive? Of course not. He only paid a small advance and then let them chase the ghost of the fake business while they ended up in court.

And the icing on the cake from the T-Rex team included a constant barrage of misinformation on various social media networks and comments sections of the local newspapers. Social media! What a wonderfully divisive and alienating medium. Liam felt the collective motto for the various platforms should read "Creators of Envy. Destroyers of Happiness." Satan himself could not have crafted a more nefarious method of sewing discontent. If claims in opposition to his development in The County were vocalized, it was easy to shout them down from behind a computer screen, labeling thoughtful arguments in favor of the environment as lies, ridiculous, and failures. And as for articles in the weekly publications, there was nothing more effective than some negative comments to take the argument off-topic and to bury the actual concerns.

To Liam Wallace, most people were suckers who were easily duped. Particularly poorly educated people. He proudly considered how he dissuaded an audience worried about water pollution by sighting statistics he made up himself, right at that moment, but no one there would question them because people believed in numbers and lists rather than having to actually calculate realities.

Liam considered the possibilities. By this time next year they would have the first few hastily built homes in place. Put a grand facade over the cheap material core. Much like the fraternity house he lived in while at college. Humans were drawn to image and not substance. Humanity's self-absorbed nature was on display more than ever with the persistent use of cell phones and the endless stream of selfie photographs. "Look at me. I'm important and doing something fabulous. Listen to me talking. I'm saying something critical."

What a simple culture to exploit, he thought to himself. Tell them what they wanted to hear and you could buy their land, their votes, their rights and self-esteem. Their aspirations ended with "Fake it 'til you make it." It was a shallow society of sheep that were easy marks for a predator like himself. Hell, he could probably get away with murder and no one would question it. In a way, he already had! The defense would be simple: Deny. Deny. Deny.

10

THE BEAR LUNAR

"Max, think you're ready for The Bear Lunar?"

I could hear Hannah calling out from her kitchen. She had been busy digging into the background of the T-Rex company, searching for connections between them and Kate's death, all the while becoming more attentive to their dealings and transactions around The County. She essentially had taken over Kate's role as a whistle blower and disrupter of their plans for—what they were marketing it as—Lakeland Estates: A gated community and private beachfront resort with a golf course, club house, pool facilities, town center, shops, grocery and unrivaled sunsets. The only line missing was, "Undesirables need not apply."

But this week Hannah's mood was entirely different and her focus continued to rotate around the forthcoming excursion to South Manitou Island. "No," I called out from the studio, "what should I be planning on?"

She walked through the sliding door and into the studio carrying two mugs of coffee, handing one of them to me. "Here, it's Higher Grounds. Justice blend. Good stuff." She continued, "This will be the ultimate final for your mentorship. But aside from that, do you get seasick? Sometimes the trip out there gets choppy if the wind is up."

The recreational occasions where I'd been on boats never involved violent conditions. Gentle rocking through a wake and occasional faster currents were the extent of my experience. "I don't think so. I've never had that uneasy, queasy feeling."

"Okay. Just checking in case you were a complete flutter belly on the water. Some people are. The slightest motion under their feet, even on a pontoon boat, can set them off. A few times I've seen people tossing up their lunch on Glen Lake in perfectly calm weather."

She returned to the talk about prep for the trip. "You'll want to bring your backpack and carry some extra layers. There's no forecast for rain—we probably would stay on the mainland if that was the case—but it can get chilly at times out there on the island. It's a late night affair and usually goes on until dawn. And you'll need to hike in some supplies for the event. I'll help you with that. It won't be dark until about 10 P.M. We typically head out from Leland in the early evening."

"How many people will be there?" Logistically it didn't sound like it could be very big.

"In the past, when the weather forecast is good like this, the south island gathering usually draws a few dozen members of our clan. Like a large house party." Hannah was sipping her coffee and sat down on one of the bar stools.

"Isn't there a concern about alarming, well, normal people camping on the island?" A large group of hikers, at night, seemed to me like it would draw attention.

"Oh, no worries," she was confident. "Our guys book the camp grounds and ferry transit years in advance. The moon phases are known, so the date is predictable. And our members work as park rangers. There are a lot more of us than you might suspect. We end up having the place to ourselves. Richard Branson couldn't have a more exclusive retreat."

I found that reassuring. But of course it would be like that. Nonetheless it seemed like a lot of work for a party. "What goes on? What should I expect?"

"Oh, there's food and drinking, a bit of ritual, and of course living as your spirit animal out in the open," Hannah was shaking her head. "You'll have to experience it for yourself."

I'd run off in the evenings on some solo excursions, walking around the forests near Glen Arbor as a bear, learning more about myself in that manner. But rarely had those lasted more than an hour. And I hadn't seen other clan members as bears with the exception of Hannah and Bern. It sounded like it would be a gathering unlike any other that I'd been to.

***

On the day of the event, a Thursday evening in mid-August, Bern pulled into the driveway ready to take us up to Leland. He owned a large, deep blue, Ford pickup with a hitch and a plow attachment in the front. The sort of vehicle that comes in handy in the winter, especially in a county that gets sixteen feet of snow on average, every winter. He was a generous neighbor and often plowed nearby resident's driveways after clearing his own. In the fall he'd move harvests of apples, cherries, grapes, pumpkins and anything else to the various markets. In springtime he transported topsoil and gardening supplies. And in summer the flatbed was often occupied by kayaks or bicycles.

It was a practical vehicle and an extension of Bern's values. Like most every member of the clan—at least what I observed about those living in The County—no one owned superfluous items or lived in lavish mansions. Being connected to the spirit world and a spirit animal left one less occupied with the trappings and clutter of the material world. Creature comforts were appreciated but you didn't need to live in a 5,000 square foot home with 5 bathrooms, 5 bedrooms, and 3,000 square feet of space you never used. It was a surplus of furnishings and a bitch of a heating bill. The clan members, as well as many non-clan residents of The County, enjoyed the outdoors year-round. Who needed a huge, empty home with a vehicle that couldn't handle the icy conditions?

For this occasion the only thing in the trailer was his backpack. He phoned in his ETA ahead of time, and Hannah and I where ready to greet him with our own gear as he walked up the drive. He gave her a big hug and me as well. They'd become like family, although I was beginning to feel I might need to find a place of my own. I'd been living in Hannah's studio and the Westie since arriving to The County months ago. Her place was inexpensive—I didn't pay rent— but I was sleeping on a sofa provided for gallery guests and didn't have a ton of personal space beyond what I kept in my own vehicle.

Ever since coming out of hibernation I held no further illusions to my initial plans to head south at the end of summer. Leelanau County had become my new home. I could continue working in Hannah's gallery but I'd need to move out eventually. She had been a welcoming mentor but she and Bern had their own life and routines.

We climbed into the cab, me hopping into the spacious back seat, and headed up M-22 towards Leland. It was a quick ride and we arrived in less than a half hour. Our final destination was Fishtown, the collection of shops, restaurants, charters and fishing boats gathered at the core of Leland's harbor along the river that emanated out of nearby Lake Leelanau. The weathered shanties and docks looked like something belonging in an Andrew Wyeth painting of a town in Maine. In the past this had truly been the core of a fishing village before the stocks of whitefish and lake trout had been fished out or decimated by the introduction of non-native species.

In the 1950s, alewives, a type of big-eyed herring from the Atlantic Ocean, found their way into the Great Lakes system via ballast water transported within the hauls of freighters using the St. Lawrence Seaway. The voracious little fish devoured the native fry and eggs and within a decade their numbers exploded into great shoals while the native fish stocks were nearly wiped out completely. To counter the alewives, Pacific salmon were introduced to the Great Lakes. The salmon effectively consumed the alewives and proliferated in growing numbers. A huge sport-fishing economy blossomed over the next couple decades until the salmon populations too, like the alewives, crashed.

Today only one commercial fishing vessel, the *Janice Sue*, operated full-time out of Leland. The others boats were pleasure craft or charters chasing after the less-abundant salmon, or ferries to the Manitou Islands.

Our private craft awaited us at the end of the dock. *El Orso Negro* was owned by Finn, the wiry, cantankerous boat captain I'd met that one evening at Dick's Pour House. There were others already on the boat. I recognized Will and Petra and a girl who looked to be about my age was with them. Must be one of their daughters, I figured. We ambled along the well-worn boards and were greeted with waving hands.

"Hey, there!" Will offered to take Hannah's bag as she jumped on deck. Finn's boat was large but six passengers was the comfortable maximum. We made the rounds of hellos. "Max, this is Lea, our daughter, the one who lives in Lansing." She stepped forward and gave me a friendly hug. Like her parents she had their dark hair and brown eyes.

"No Charlotte?" I heard Bern asking.

"No. She had a big project to deal with at work and couldn't get away," said Will.

"She's turning into a regular New Yorker."

"Except that she lives in D.C."

"Oh, that's right. Well, East Coast. High fashion. Fast-paced. You know what I mean."

I was trying to be casual but admittedly I was checking out Lea. She looked adventurous and fun, if such traits can be perceived at first sight. We all were dressed like we were going out for a day hike on a hot summer day. Boots. Cargo shorts. T-shirts printed with Michigan themes like *Great Lakes, Unsalted and Shark-Free*. Lea in a plaid patterned top.

"ALRIGHT. EVERYBODY GOOD?" Finn's voice cracked through the air. He was smoking a cigarette while readying to untie the boat from the cleats along the dock. He was a unique character amongst clan members. Most were a health-conscious, anti-smoking lot but here was a guy with an independent outlook. It was his life to do what he wanted, and to hell with your opinion on the matter. He was a good-hearted person who took a while getting used to.

The boat pulled off from the dock and we were on our way, Finn piloting the boat while the six of us opted to stand outside taking in the view. "There's beer in the cooler." Finn informed us while I was about to check out one of the long fishing poles he had attached along the cabin. "And goddamnit don't fuck with my fishing lines!" His voice was sharp. My hand shot back like it was slapped. Bern, Will, Petra and Hannah just looked bemused. "Not even five minutes in and you're already getting ornery," Bern teased with a jesting call.

Hannah popped open the cooler and started handing out beers. "We've got about an hour to ride. Finn, you want one?"

"Is the Pope Catholic?"

She handed the beer can to Will who tossed it over to Finn, now with the wheel on cruise control. Fishtown gradually faded away. It felt as if we were riding out into the open ocean. In the distance you could see the Manitous but the far-off horizon was nothing but water. To our left—or port, I should say—on the mainland were the giant dunes of Pyramid Point, a prominent landmark rising more than 300 feet above the shoreline, that had been referenced for centuries in navigating these straits.

Fortunately the winds were calm and the cruise was about as

rough as crossing a pond on a golf course. The motion of the boat provided a welcomed breeze to the humid August afternoon.

"So, we've got our first-timer with us," Hannah was motioning to me. Being on the water, secluded and away from the usual population was already feeling different.

"Yes. And I'm not entirely sure what to expect. Although I still find it difficult to believe that we end up having the place to ourselves," I emphasized "to ourselves" with air quotes.

"Our clan has been living in this place for a long while, now. We've got our angles covered." Bern spoke with casual confidence.

"This park didn't happen entirely by chance. And the inclusion of the islands was very intentional. Elders like Finn here and others volunteer each Lunar so we can all experience it at least once. No ferries will be running regular tourists today. They're "booked" (air quotes again) with our members. And our friends in the Coast Guard and at the Ranger station dissuade private craft from mooring off the beaches. Sure, it becomes increasingly difficult to coordinate as more and more people move to the area, but we'll continue until it cannot be safely conducted." Bern took a swig from his beer can, "And we always have the mosquitoes on our side."

"Mosquitoes?" I asked. That was a rather tangent addendum.

"Yes, they can be awful on the island," Petra filled in, "which is great for us. Nature's deterrent to overnight campers."

"How is that not terrible for us as well?"

"Oh, do you get eaten alive?" she sounded surprised.

I had to think about it. Not really. Sure, I'd get a bite every now and them but never swarmed like most people I knew. In Minnesota, mosquitoes could be so numerous they'd been in the running for the official state bird but lost in a contested vote to the black flies. "No, I don't. But I figured I was just lucky."

"It's a trait. Their saliva doesn't irritate us. Perhaps that's the entire reason we evolved to have a relation with a spirit animal, just to avoid the damn mosquitoes!" Petra's laugh was jovial. You wanted people like her, that energy, at a party.

We'd been pacing along, with the island looming larger as we neared. Finn continued chain smoking, listening to our conversations, interjecting with the occasional joking remarks such as, "Mosquitoes are like family. Annoying, but they carry your blood." Followed by his cackling laugh.

I was taking it all in as we approached our destination, the dock at the South Manitou Island Lighthouse. The imposing structure stood out like a sentinel overlooking the passage between the island and Pyramid Point. Finn guided in the boat like he'd done it a thousand times. Bern and Will jumped out to help with the lines. We each gathered up our backpacks and climbed out, pounding down beers as if we couldn't bring them along.

"Finn, aren't you coming?" I thought he'd be joining us.

"No, you kids enjoy yourself," he responded. "I'm here to make sure there's an exit strategy in case somebody needs one. I'll hang back and do some fishing while you get all natural."

"You're such a gentleman, Finn," Bern was saying. "How is it you've stayed a bachelor all these years?"

"Do you all have your *moon vision*?" Finn asked, as a mother might remind a child to have their gloves on a cold winter day. I had an idea of what he was talking about, although I wasn't entirely sure. Hannah had packed our bags with water, a bed sheet that I later learned was cut for use as a toga, and a suspect bottle of something. Everyone indicated yes except for me.

"Max the first-timer. You ain't looking too sure," he was saying.

"Oh, he's all set," Hannah assured.

"Nonetheless, kid. Take this. Share it before the gathering." Finn was handing me a small steel flask. "Trust me. It's better than whatever she cooked up," he nodded toward Hannah, "unless she had some helpful ingredients from Blue."

Hannah stepped forward and gave Finn a big smooch on the cheek. "Thanks, you old bastard. Love you. See you at dawn," she said.

I grabbed the flask and thanked him. And with that we set foot on the island.

***

Almost immediately we spotted a couple of bears loping off into the woods on the periphery.

"Looks like some folks are getting started early," Will observed. "I can't recognize who that is from here."

"Some people like to make a full day of it. I don't know how they handle the following morning," Petra added.

"What's the general plan?" I asked. "And what's with the moon vision? It sounds like we all have moonshine."

"Moon vision affects you only when you're in bear form, Max," Hannah said in her instructor's voice. "Think of it as liquid happiness. Not drunk but just—groovy. A decent gulp will keep you feeling it for an hour or so. Take a slug before you change over. And give Finn's a try. He can be crafty with his ingredients."

Bern resumed, "As for the general plan, we're heading straight to the party. This year's coordinators will have stocked the barns well ahead of time. There'll be plenty of libations and snacks. It's an event celebrating us. Our clan. An appreciation of the environment we cultivate and protect. And a reverence to the balance that makes it all possible."

"And it's a party," Will stated flatly.

"But we're early enough that you and Lea should hike out to see the old-growth cedar trees before it's time to gather at the Farm," Petra added. "They're impressive and worth the excursion. Lea, you remember the trail out there from the last time, right?"

I suddenly felt like I was being set up on a date. But the beer and the boat ride already instilled a come-as-it-may mindset.

"Yeah, I remember," Lea was saying. "They are super-cool. Come on, Max. I'll lead the way. We'll see you all again in a few hours. Dusk at the latest."

We parted ways with the "parents"—which is how I found myself mentally referring to Hannah and Bern—them heading up the beach while Lea and I started out on a trail following the southern part or the island. She was sociable and the hike wasn't awkward at all. And I certainly didn't mind the view as she forged ahead along the path in boots and shorts showing off toned legs and a body that looked more active than average.

"Are you a runner?" I asked while following.

"Oh. Sorry if I move quickly. And actually, yes, I do enjoy running, and pretty much any activity outdoors," answered Lea.

"I don't mind the pace at all. I'm used to it from biking all the time. So…" I hadn't really spent time with a clan family, "what was it like growing up in a house where you're parents knew about having a spirit animal?" I'd been wondering ever since we got on the boat, watching Lea interacting with Will and Petra.

She slowed to be more alongside of me. "I have you at an advantage. My parents filled me in on your background, your arrival to Leelanau County, and the tattoo on your hand from Blue."

She pointed, "Look out for that poison ivy." Tendrils of the three-leafed vine were spread out to the right, wound around a fallen branch. We sidestepped the itchy plant. Lea put her hand on my shoulder as we ambled over some exposed roots.

"Anyhow, my experience growing up was pretty average—at first. You've met my parents. They were completely open with my sister and I. When Charlotte learned to connect with the spirit world—well, it's like with any first child. When it was my turn three years later, they could anticipate my needs almost before I could ask. And it was strange how at one point you just *know*."

"How was it having a sibling around?" Being an only child, my frame of reference was vague. And the question was even more curious considering you could change into a bear.

"As with any brother or sister you have a common bond. And ours was particularly special. Once we were both old enough to change it evoked a bit of recklessness," Lea mischievously suggested. "We'd take road trips engaging in behaviors we probably wouldn't pursue had it not been for the knowledge that we could turn into bears if we were ever forced into a bad situation."

"Did that ever happen?" I thought back to the first time Hannah revealed herself to me, and I damn near had a heart attack. Besides, it was an unspoken rule within the clan that using your abilities in that manner was a last resort option.

"Thankfully, no. But you can imagine? Even if you change for just a few seconds you would probably freak someone out big time. They'd be questioning their sanity."

We were rounding a bend and a ghostly large object appeared on the water. "What's that ship doing out there?" I asked.

We paused at the overlook and Lea filled me in with a quick history lesson without even referencing the informative sign.

"That's the same thing I thought the first time I saw that two years ago. It's the wreck of the *Francisco Morazan*, an ocean freighter originally built a long time ago in Germany. Even the Nazis used it. Over the years it changed hands. And during a late November snowstorm in 1960—queue that *Edmond Fitzgerald* song—it wrecked upon the shoal out there. None of the crew were lost. They just stayed on board until they could be rescued. But the ship became a total loss."

"A spirit of its former self," I added. "It would be fun to paddle-board out there. Very surreal."

As we continued toward the cedars, Lea asked, "Speaking of surreal, what was it like meeting Blue? She's a real one-of-a-kind." Lea was sizing me up, taking a look at my tattoo. I'd come to realize that my encounter carried a mystique about it. Like I'd seen a vintage rock band at a small venue before they became big. Fellow clan members always asked about it.

"I'm grateful for her taking me in. Without that encounter I wouldn't be here talking with you." I caught myself too late, realizing with that statement that I'd exposed my hand. Lea was swaying me with her easy-going charm.

She gave me an amused grin and I returned to the subject of spirit bears.

"Blue gave me some psychedelic honey. That was her way of gently introducing me to who we are. Hannah says the honey was probably a concoction derived from the spirit world. She also thinks Blue walked me through that dimension when she returned me to my Westie that night. But I can't recall it. Only obscure, fleeting images. Like a dream."

Lea's face looked intrigued. "That would be crazy. I don't know of anyone spending an extended time in the spirit world. Although it's alongside us in the material world all the time."

Like I was saying, the encounter had an aspect of glamour.

"Aren't there other spirit bears in the clan?" I wondered.

"My parents say there are, sometimes. But Blue is the only one I know of. The analogy they told me was it's like a white buffalo. You know, when a herd suddenly has an all-white calf. Native

Americans assigned a sacred significance to white buffalos." Lea's example was spot-on. "And in our clan a spirit bear is like having an ambassador to the spirit world. Amusing to think fate presented that in the form of a woman. She must be incredibly powerful with her abilities and knowledge."

We reached the grove of old-growth cedars the park referred to as the Valley of the Giants. For trees in the Midwest, these were giants, some over 500 years old. It was difficult to imagine that the forests of Michigan used to look like this everywhere. The atmosphere felt different, primal. Clan members living in the region at that time likely enjoyed a bountiful arrangement with the environment. These trees were living reminders of the balance with nature we aspired to achieve. It must have been traumatic to watch the logging industry of the past destroy in years what took centuries to create.

It makes you consider, "What is progress?" Technical innovations, satellite communication, expedient travel, vaccinations—all wondrous advances. But so often they are at the expense of our place and connection with the animals and plants in the world. You'd think that humanity could be smart enough to achieve equilibrium with both.

We wandered around looking up, eventually looping back to the main trail. Surprisingly, we didn't encounter other fellow Bear Lunar participants. "They're probably all up at the farm. But we have time. Let's check out the dunes overlook. It's a half-mile away." Lea gave me a slight shove in the direction of the dunes. We neared the overlook in a matter of minutes.

"So, Max," Lea's voice changed to playful, "what do you look like?"

"What, like this?"

"No. As a bear. We'll all see each other later. You'll never see so many bears in one location. The party really gets going, then. Especially under the full moon. But let's see what we look like, now." Lea slipped off her backpack, then her boots, then… I had to suppress my body's reaction. She looked unbelievable. Before she changed she beckoned, "Come, on, Max. Let's see it." And there she was, transformed into a bear, staring at me.

Of course, I obliged. I watched her as I stripped off my clothes and changed over, reading her eyes. And with that she ran off toward the overlook. I pursued, catching up and bumping her along the sand. Being playful in bear form was something I hadn't experienced. It felt raw and alive. She rolled over, stood up, and weighed into me, rolling me back. We tussled in the sand but paused at one point to take in the view. Two bears overlooking the incredible blue and green hues beyond the dunescape. She slipped back into human form so she could talk. I did so as well. "It's beautiful, don't you think?" she questioned.

"Yes it is." But I was looking at her. We moved together and kissed. My eagerness was obvious now, but she waived me off. "Not here, Max. Sex in this sand would be awful." But she was grinning, knowing full well how enchanted I was with her. "Besides, wait until we drink some of that moon vision. It'll show you where you're at. Or at least it'll help you really feel it."

I stepped into her arms. "We don't have to roll around in the sand."

***

Lea and I doubled back to the farm, hiking along the west side of Florence Lake, and arrived just before dusk. As we approached, we could hear continuous drumbeats like the bass line at a dance club. The scene looked like nature's version of Studio 54. There were tiki torches, people drinking, standing around wrapped in togas, bears milling about, troughs of moon vision-laced honey mead were scattered around the grounds, as were the drummers. Lea and I walked into the clearing of the farm grounds and scanned the crowd for Will, Petra, Bern and Hannah. We spotted them across the open field in a mix with other people I hazily recognized.

"Hey there!" I could hear Hannah calling out. She and the others were all dressed in togas like they belonged in the Roman Senate.

"What's with the outfits?" I asked Lea as we strolled over to the group.

"It's a lot more practical for quick changing from human to bear. The previous Bear Lunar I was a senior in college. Charlotte was with me that time. And there were a few other people our age at this gathering. Admittedly it can be a bit weird partying with the older folks in this setting but there really aren't alternatives for all-out bear events. The moon vision takes the edge off in bear form and there are plenty of drink options for when you're in human form."

"What did you think of the cedars," Petra asked, as we approached, "aren't they marvelous?"

"Yes, they were well worth the hike. You simply don't see trees like that very often. We also walked out to the dunes," I added without divulging the rest.

"Well get yourselves something to drink and toss on some togas," Bern directed. "The gathering should take place in just a little while."

The Conrad Hutzler Farm was a collection of old structures, some dating back to the 1800s, and was for a time an active working farm for some of South Manitou's early residents. It was incorporated with the park but tonight it served as party central. Provisions for the event, beers, food and so forth were stored here ahead of time. Backpacks from others lined the wall of one of the old barns. We placed ours among them and each pulled out our makeshift bed sheet togas. Hannah had packed mine with a ceramic clasp she must have designed in her studio. It was a bear's head etched on the face of a moon. Lea's had a wooden pin in the shape of a paw.

"Oh, and let's drink some of the stuff Finn gave you," Lea said as she slipped over her toga and tied a loose cord around her waste.

The outfits weren't high fashion but they were practical. We both took a long pull off the flask that Finn gave me. It tasted like herbal honey but finished smooth and sweet, almost like ice cream.

"What's in this stuff, do you know?" I asked Lea, returning the flask to my backpack.

"I don't know. I've not learned how to make it. They have communal batches in the small wooden troughs. They're like punch bowls. But Finn's has a far more interesting flavor."

We grazed at one of the food tables, nodding hellos and engaging in idle banter with other members. After hiking all evening we were craving some calories. We grabbed a drink of mead from a keg and rejoined the group. Other clan members had started to assemble in the clearing as well, everyone now in human form and wearing togas of various designs. As if instructed, everyone started to form a large, loose circle. There were about 60 people, most slightly older than us, a few our age, everyone looking like a participant at the start of a bizarre theatrical play. A woman stepped out to the center of the ring, calling everyone's attention.

"Thank you all for coming out tonight to celebrate The Bear Lunar. For those members who don't know me, I'm Rebecca, the clan's resident archivist and this year's Conductor here on South Manitou." There was a smattering of cheers from folks who did indeed know her.

Rebecca continued, "I'll keep it short. We gather every other year on The Bear Lunar to reconvene as a clan, rejoice in our shared abilities, and to recognize one another in our spirit animal form. We hold our own set of truths to be self-evident. That a balance with the environment in this world correlates to a balanced connection with the spirit world. We can live sensibly in a community that doesn't exploit its natural resources. Enjoying our common talent makes us all collectively stronger. Some of you have been here before. For others it is your first time. So let us greet each other as our spirit animal and reinforce the bonds that bring us together."

And with that Rebecca tossed aside her toga while slipping into her bear form. Others followed suit and within moments we were all bears. It was dizzying. I'd never experienced such a feeling of belonging. People—I mean bears—began to amble about, sniffing, brushing up against themselves, saying hellos. The drummers had stopped when the circle had formed and a strange silence was broken by the shuffling sounds made by dozens of bears. But at the same time I could feel something more intense than my usual self as a bear. The moon vision started to bend my awareness. Gradually things became more colorful. My senses were more acute. A calming ecstasy was slowly coursing through my veins and it appeared almost everyone else experienced something similar. I perceived no aggression in the crowd, only warmth and kindness.

Hannah and Bern momentarily nuzzled my ears. Will and Petra nodded. I was aware of Lea mingling with the crowd alongside me. All the while my heightened senses were registering the scents and physical traits of my fellow clan members. After tonight I'd be able to identify them even if I didn't necessarily know their names. The carousing continued as the night slowly set in and the moon began to glow against the darkened sky.

Bears started to pair off or depart in groups to experience the wilderness, open and freely, unencumbered by outside surveillance. Others changed back into humans, naked and embracing. Some of the drummers returned to human form and resumed the rhythmic pounding. The farm suddenly had a charged, bacchanal ambiance. I felt a tug at my shoulder. Lea was motioning for me to follow. She trotted down a road leading out to the west side of the island. Others were doing the same. We emerged from the woods and sprinted out across the sand dunes bathing in moonlight. In the periphery you could see other bears and humans doing the same. Lea ran down the incline, onto the beach and into the water. I bounded in after her and changed back to human form so we could talk. She did the same. We both agreed that a couple more degrees in water temperature would be welcomed. The soft sand below the shallow, clear water glistened. She dove under and surfaced in front me, wrapping her arms around my neck.

***

The night went on, gathering with others in bear form, as the moon cast a spectral light on the festivities.

As with all parties, the energy began to wane and people returned to wearing togas or readying themselves for the return trip. I felt like I gained an entire town of new friends. At the crack of dawn everyone began to circle back to the dock. All the refuse was flammable. No bottles, or plastics, or empty cans. Clan members remaining behind would burn up all the evidence in the coming hours. Many were boarding the waiting ferries. A few other groups also had charters piloted by an elder.

We all piled onto Finn's boat. He was already up, smoking a cigarette and greeting us with his morning catchphrase, "The sun is up and the eagles are singing." We all took a seat this time. I put my arm around Lea. It was obvious to Will and Petra that I'd be seeing more of them in the future. I think that was part of their plan all along.

"You guys look like hell," Finn was smiling as he untied the last rope to the dock. "It must have been a good time."

11

COUNTER MEASURES

"They're empty communities that offer nothing in return."

Hannah was addressing the informal crowd, once again gathered at Dick's Pour House, expressing concerns about the impending T-Rex development south of Leland. Since the Bear Lunar, she had been dedicating substantial amounts of time to digging up news reports and stories about the company's dealings in Texas and elsewhere throughout the county. Dick's Pour House may as well been referred to as the county seat instead of the actual facilities in Suttons Bay. Its central location and favorable amenities like beer on tap gave it an advantage over the formally recognized entity. With the clan's involvement in so much of The County government, one could argue—and rightfully so—that the real decisions and votes that mattered happened here, under dingy lighting at tables lined with pitchers.

"Sometimes the homes, condos and townhouses end up serving as investment harbors for the CEOs of foreign corporations, usually the corrupt ones, from countries involved in terrible human rights violations." She was like a coach outlining a big play.

"So, you mean they're investors from the United States?" someone quipped, "or maybe they're from *Crook* County Illinois."

Hannah ignored the jokes, even if they were accurate. "Think about it. You're members of a mafia, organized crime, or a dictator's inner circle, whatever. You need a place to bank your assets. Someplace where the value won't plummet and tracing the ownership can be concealed behind fake personas or shell enterprises. Welcome to the real estate holdings of T-Rex. They take the money in return for guaranteed initial investments and inflated values even though no one actually resides in them."

Her point might seemed far-fetched, but she was preaching to a group who, in a way, were a mafia—albeit one favorable to the community and environment. "I've been finding reports from Texas, Florida, various locations along the East Coast—anywhere these guys operate—and the results always end up being negative. People get pushed out. Traffic worsens. Local businesses replaced by chains and box stores. Local character and identity is lost. Increased water pollution. Light pollution. Old growth forests and open land replaced by golf courses and parking lots." Hannah was rolling.

"Sounds like some folks' definition of patriotism," someone added. "Pave over trees. Drive everywhere. Get fat. Live off pharmaceuticals. Blame your unhappiness on other people."

Hannah continued, "Even the initial benefits of providing construction work in the area are negligible. They hire suppliers who are part of their own network. The materials are cheap. They pay wages with zero benefits and the contracts with locals are marginal."

"How is it they're so profitable? Seems like consumers would eventually learn." That was from the end of the table.

"Like traveling salesmen in the past, selling snake oil. There's always a new community to approach that's never heard of them. That's why they're up here in Michigan. They've burned a lot of bridges elsewhere. They take the money and run, never paying taxes, writing off decreases in property values as losses. If we let them get their project off the ground we'll be left with their trash to clean up and a bankruptcy filings," Hannah concluded.

"Well, then what to do to stop them?" Finn's familiar voice sounded through the commotion. "Haven't they been blocked from obtaining the necessary permits?"

"That hasn't been slowing them down," Hannah cited. "Kate's passing opened up a new opportunity to fill a commissioner seat favorable to the T-Rex development. And I'll get back to that in just a moment," she stated ominously. "They're probably responsible for cutting down that tract of old-growth trees slated for protection that was inconveniently located right where they want to build."

Mentioning the downed trees brought a groaning murmur among the group. The news of them being "harvested"—at night, without public input—had produced bad vibes throughout The County. People were suspicious of who was responsible. Suspects were being manufactured along with news that the contractors were from out of state. The T-Rex company had plenty of motive to have the trees removed, but so might others, and there wasn't any definitive evidence connecting them to "the crime" which is how the clan members viewed it.

"Well, winter will definitely stall any immediate plans for building," that declaration came from Tom, the burly Leland resident whom I recognized from the first meeting back in spring. He was a quiet yet consistent presence at meetings and events. "A couple months from now we'll probably have a foot of snow on the ground. And in the meantime we can come up with a new strategy to derail the project."

Hannah took a deep, calming breath before her next comment. "That's true, Tom. But there's another matter that we need to look into," she glanced around the bar taking in the crowd dynamics. "Kate's death might not have been an accident. Some T-Rex goons, under direction from that Liar Wallace, are likely responsible for rigging her car to swerve off the road, causing the fatal crash."

A questioning silence answered her until someone asked, "What proof do you have of that? And what made you come up with that idea anyway?"

"Max here overheard them bragging about it one evening while having a meal at Sleder's," Hannah was talking but all eyes at the table swerved over to my direction. I probably looked like a deer in the headlights. "And I've been trying to determine if that sort of thing would even be possible. And it is. Not like Kate owned a car with a modern computer that could be hacked. This would be more like a one-time "detonation" using a wireless component where a critical feature gets disabled—provided you had access to the car ahead of time to install the device with the trigger. If you search the internet enough you can find instructions and even videos with suggestions on how to do it."

I was then put on the spot to re-tell what I had overheard that fateful night at Sleder's, how the intention of the T-Rex agents was to scare Kate off but her death was treated like a bonus arrangement. I then mentioned how it all came together with the drive-by sighting of their vehicle at Kate's memorial party.

The mood of the gathering was shifting from concern to anger, with cooler heads attempting to reason with the facts available. The talks continued, now focused on any community buzz that might support news of meddlesome or curious activities.

When the meeting adjourned everyone was in agreement that further evidence would be needed before pursuing any retaliation for Kate's death, but adopting a policy of resistance, protest and sounding an alarm to the public now and throughout the winter would be of utmost importance in order to counter any further advancements by the T-Rex people. Some, like Tom, volunteered to be in attendance at all county hearings in an attempt to sway the commissioners. Others would go door-to-door to talk to neighbors and landowners in the area targeted for development south of Leland. Hannah said she would contact our clan members in law enforcement to comb over the report involving Kate's death. And I offered to post comments and letters to local publications in opposition of the T-Rex dealings. We departed with our marching orders and felt confident of being able to successfully block the deal.

***

That night I rode back to Glen Arbor with Hannah and Bern. Pondering our odds, I asked, "What percentage of Leelanau County residents are members of our clan?"

"We do keep our own census, loosely. Rebecca, our main archivist—well, you met her at the Bear Lunar," Bern reminded me of the Conductor of Ceremonies, "she'd know for sure. And the land use keeps the population growth to a minimum compared to a more urban setting like Traverse City. So, figure around half. Well, half of the adults. Not sure about kids." He turned from the passenger seat to look back. "Speaking of you younger folks, have you been keeping in touch with Lea?"

Bern was asking the obvious. Of course I had been. She and I hung out the weekend following the night of the Bear Lunar. She stayed with her parents in Suttons Bay and I'd drive over in the Westie. We'd toss bikes onto the rack and would take excursions along the remote stretches of road north of Northport. Up there, the Kehl Lake area was nice for secluded hiking. We'd slip off the trail and into the rest of the small forest preserve, changing over as bears, feeling completely in touch with nature and each other. At this point I couldn't imagine a different lifestyle, being with someone outside of the clan. How would anyone understand?

And Lea felt the same way. Her job in Lansing was with the Department or Natural Resources. They managed forests, rivers, recreational areas, and issued fishing and hunting licenses. Some residents—particularly hunters and fishermen—considered them a common nuisance. She planned to transfer her credentials to a job in The County. We'd talk and wonder if there were other clans like ours elsewhere.

"Well, that's the trip that Blue decided to take. Like Lewis and Clark on a voyage of discovery," Lea reminded me. I was surprised there weren't more of us in the Upper Peninsula. But then, considering the true Legend of the Sleeping Bears, the crossing of Lake Michigan landed our clan in what eventually became Leelanau County, and that's where we stayed.

"Oh, look. He's blushing," Hannah heckled me with eyes in the rearview mirror. Not that she could clearly see my face.

"Yeah," I confessed, "you got me. I'm still seeing Lea and plan on doing so for a long while. I might go visit her in Lansing after Labor Day. Hannah you wouldn't mind me taking a few days away from the studio, would you?"

"Not at all, kid. But it's that Westie I'm concerned about. Do you think that old roller could make it downstate and back?"

"Well, I was going to ask if I could borrow your Subaru…?" My voice trailed with a questioning high note.

"Damn, that kid has got it bad," Bern said to Hannah, the "it" being my crush on Lea.

"Yeah, sure, Max. You can take my car. But you'll need to leave me the keys to the Westie in case I need to run some errands around town."

"Thanks. You're the best." I floated out another idea, "I'm also starting to think I should find a place of my own."

"Hey! Sounds like you're planning to stay put, eh?" Hannah commented. "You're welcome to stay at my place, Max. Rents in town aren't exactly cheap."

"I appreciate the offer. And I'll take you up on it until I can find something. But, yeah—no more plans of heading south. I think I'll be staying for a long while. Besides, Lea mentioned possibly finding a job up here in The County."

From the back seat I could see Hannah and Bern looking at each other, smiling in the dashboard light, like cupids who knew they'd arranged a successful romance.

12

Playing with Fire

L iam Wallace was pacing back and forth around his office, enraged. "What the hell is happening? It's like we've kicked a beehive."

He'd been getting phone calls from "concerned citizens"—those bothersome types who think they should have a say as to what gets built in their neighborhood. Suddenly, county commissioners were caring about details with regard to the Lakeland Estates development. Details! Who reads the fine print? The complete terms of an agreement? No one does.

And there were articles, comments and letters to the editor in local news publications asking questions and proposing arguments in opposition to his plans.

"Why are people paying attention now?" Liam was asking his associates gathered around his desk. "We had this on cruise control. Residents pitted against each other. Their total acceptance of suspicion and lies. We were at a point where I felt confident we'd be able to sell these Michigan chumps their own water."

Which coincidentally is something the State of Michigan already agreed to with a foreign company called Nestlé, headquartered on Lake Geneva, far away in Switzerland. Nestlé bought the rights to pump spring water from aquifers in Michigan, which they then bottled in plastic and sold back to the residents who granted them the power to do so. Ironically, those same bottles were then supplied to the town of Flint, Michigan, when it turned out the city's water lines were poisonously contaminated with lead.

"There's a woman named Hannah who's been stirring up trouble," said one of the associates. "She's been a principal agitator. I hear she's even contacted law enforcement to re-examine the auto accident." He didn't have to say which auto accident. Everyone in the room knew he was talking about Kate.

"Jesus Christ!" For some people, Jesus was akin to God. Others wouldn't know him from Adam. Liam wasn't invoking the name in an exalted manner. He was angry. "So that's why I got that call from the Sheriff's department to 'clarify some statements'."

He turned to the two men he was with at Sleder's, the same one's who had fatally rigged Kate's car.

"We need to do something about this Hannah woman. Cut the head off the snake before it constricts this entire project. We've worked too hard. We're in the red zone about to score. We cannot fumble away this opportunity." Liam was fond of football analogies despite the fact he never participated in team sports.

"Well, maybe we occupy her time with more pressing matters," one of the men stated flatly.

Liam looked up at the ceiling, pondering the options. "Yes. That would get her off our backs. But not the auto accident approach. Too conspicuous to do that twice."

At times like these he'd stroke his mustache in contemplation. "Does she have a garage? Garage fires always seem benign. Gas cans and such lying about. Oily rags. Exposed outlets."

"We could do that," answered one of the men.

"Excellent. Go forth with that plan. No need to let me know when it's done but sometime in the next couple of days. Time is of the essence." Liam reached into a desk drawer and pulled out an envelop of cash as if he anticipated paying-off people at any moment. Some people have emergency money at home to post bail. Liam had emergency cash for bribes. "Here's an advance bonus for you. There will be the other half when the job is finished."

Liam then laughed a little at his humorous spin on an old adage. "When your house is on fire, you don't care about the neighbors."

***

On a weekday evening, Hannah and Bern drove into Traverse City to have dinner at a restaurant in the Old State Hospital, now collectively referred to as The Commons. "Try dining at the Old Insane Asylum" didn't have the same marketing appeal. The sprawling campus that once catered to mentally ill patients now housed art galleries, shops, restaurants, a winery, coffee house, bakery, and of course a brewpub.

The patient rooms and administrative offices, now renovated into condos, were very popular despite persistent stories of haunted passageways and wayward specters. I had visited the grounds earlier in the summer on one of my rides. Earthen Ales, the brewpub, was ideally situated near a network of wooded trails offering light hiking, and provided some of the best beers in town for the return loop.

With the two of them out and having Hannah's place to myself, I decided to practice some of my bear skills, slinking around the woods behind the house. Your senses, especially smell and hearing, are much stronger. And that's when I heard the approaching vehicle pulling up to the studio. We were closed and it definitely didn't sound like Hannah and Bern returning to retrieve some forgotten item. I ambled back, curious to see who might be arriving, while maintaining a low profile.

The car was an automotive eyesore. An old Ford Tempo

complete with a rusted exterior, as if it had risen from the grave
of a junkyard. I didn't know how a car like that could still be
roadworthy. They never were in the first place. But I recognized the
occupants right away. I'd seen them at Sleder's and in the T-Rex
pickup truck. I didn't understand what they were doing driving
around in such a dilapidated car. Why were they here? An uneasy
feeling settled over me.

From my vantage point I watched as each man exited the car
and headed toward the back entrance of the studio with purposeful
strides. "Damnit," I thought to myself. The back door was unlocked.
Were they breaking in? I considered charging onto the scene as a
bear. My clothes were in the studio. I didn't want to come storming
in as a naked human, demanding to know what was going on. I was
on the verge of action, but within minutes they exited, apparently
with nothing, jumped back into the Tempo and calmly drove off
back in the direction from where they came.

But I could smell a change in the air. Something was smoldering.
Nearby grill? No. Holy shit! They had started a fire!

I ran through the back entrance, transformed into a human and
stood there assessing the situation. Flames were licking up the wall
in the kitchen of the house, like a grease fire. I ran over to where
I had left my clothes and quickly tossed on a pair of jeans and a
t-shirt. What the hell was this going to look like? I was going to
be the primary suspect of starting this fire. Smoke started to creep
across the ceiling. Where was my phone! I remembered Hannah
kept a fire extinguisher on one side of the pantry but the flames
were spreading quickly and retrieving the extinguisher was already
no longer an option. I decided to close the large sliding door
between the home and the studio and rushed over to the wall where
my phone was charging. My heart was pounding. Moments ago I
was happily milling around and now I was placing a panicked call
to 9-1-1.

***

The fire department wasn't far away and responded quickly. But the house ended up being a total loss and the smoke damage to the entire structure was irreversible. Right after calling 9-1-1, I called Hannah's phone. No answer. I left a message. They were probably seated at dinner. Hannah and Bern weren't the type of people to take obnoxious, loud, self-absorbed phone calls in a public setting. I dialed Bern's phone and left a message as well. Separate calls from me would get their attention.

Eventually they showed up to the scene of flashing lights and a shell of what had once been a home. I'd been telling the authorities—some who I recognized as part of our clan—that I'd been out of the house when the fire started. Which was true. Although in my version I was reading a book in the Westie when I smelled something burning and ran into the house to discover the kitchen on fire. I included my decision to close off the door between the house and studio.

"Possibly an electrical failure, a spark landing in an unfortunate location," was the response. "Some of the items in the studio might be salvaged, but that's unlikely."

When Hannah and Bern pulled up their faces displayed a surprising lack of anguish. Perhaps it was the shock. "What the hell happened?" Bern was asking me. I retold my version of the story and left it at that but Hannah could tell something wasn't right. "What a mess," was all she could say. "At least the vehicles weren't lost. Guess we'll be sleeping a Bern's tonight. We'll head over there after filing the reports so we can claim the insurance. Max, you can follow in the Westie. What a pain in the ass. I'll have to set up a temporary residence for winter."

The site was thoroughly doused and then cordoned off with the ubiquitous yellow tape. Insurance assessors would arrive in the morning. Curious passersby and enforcement officials gradually left the scene as dusk arrived. Once alone, the three of us wandered the perimeter trying to determine if anything could be recovered.

"Looks like a total loss to me," Bern was addressing Hannah. "I'm so sorry. At least our homes are separate. You can live with me until things get cleared up. Same for you and that Westie, Max." It was nice to be included.

"Yeah, I suppose you're right. Not that I owned much in terms of things I can't replace," Hannah was absently replying. She then directed at me, "Max, what are you leaving out?" Her stare scared me. I hated lying to her even if my initial motive wasn't totally clear to myself. I simply didn't feel like it would have been prudent to mention two men entering the house, setting it on fire. What was I to say? Oh, yes officer, I was in bear form watching it all happen.

"I've been waiting until we were alone," I conceded. "It was the same goons from T-Rex that I saw at Sleder's and then in the pickup that afternoon at Kate's. They showed up in an old junker car. They snuck in the house for a moment, returned to the car, took-off heading back east, and the next thing I knew the house was on fire."

"What, did they just break-in while you were there?" Bern was justifiably perplexed and surprised by this revelation.

"I was in bear form in the back woods, testing out my senses," I admitted, lamely. "And for some reason I didn't want to mention seeing those two men to the authorities. I felt I'd get tripped up trying to describe where I'd been. I couldn't admit to being in bear form, and it happened so fast it would be just as believable to have said Santa Claus walked into the house to set it on fire." Not that I had anything against Santa. "I hope I didn't screw up."

Hannah and Bern stood there in silence for a moment, contemplating the new evidence. "Are you positive it was them?" Hannah asked.

"Dead certain."

"Hmmm. You're not mentioning them may end up being for the best," Bern was planning, you could tell by his gestures. "It simplifies matters, not involving the public authorities."

"What do you mean?" I wondered how that made things less complicated.

"Easy. I'm going to confront that son-of-a-bitch Wallace tonight. And that will be the end of it." At that moment, Bern's jaw was set like he could bite nails in half.

***

"Hold on, Bern," Hannah's tone was leery, "don't go doing anything to expose our clan." Notably she didn't say, "Don't do it." Somewhere in her mind she felt like Bern's actions—whatever they might be—would be justified.

"It's now or never, Hannah," Bern determined. "He's not expecting it. He's behind killing Kate. And now burning down your house! What else is he responsible for? Where else might it lead if he's not stopped?"

"Max, you're coming with me," Bern barked it out like a drill sergeant. It was an order I wasn't about to question. "We'll take the Subaru. I know where that bastard lives and has his office. It's late. He'll be home. Hannah, take the Westie to my place. We'll meet up there when we're done."

"You boys be careful," said Hannah. "Don't do anything that I wouldn't do."

With little thought to preparation—not that we could retrieve anything useful from a burned-down house—Bern and I were driving along the two-lanes, the Subaru's headlights illuminating the road in front of us. We were taking side-roads, and being nighttime in The County, we were alone on our journey. Bern swung the car onto a gravel road.

"This leads to nowhere but it will be a safe place to park the car. I know the owner. He's one of us. He's got all sorts of blueberries, blackberries, raspberries back here. But those seasons are well past. It'll be empty. The T-Rex office is about a mile though the woods but we can cross through it easily as bears." I realized he'd thought of this route before the incident with Hannah's home.

"Hannah and I always keep canvas bags in our cars for excursions like this. We'll toss our clothes and belongings into the bag ahead of time and I'll carry them in my mouth. When we get to Wallace's place we can transform back into human form if need be."

We parked, undressed, stuffed our shoes and clothes into the bag and took off as bears through the woods with Bern leading the way. You could smell a bit of decay setting in. Autumn was coming. We rambled across the rolling terrain of gullies and ditches. This would have been brutal to cross as a human.

In a short while we spotted the T-Rex home and office of Liam Wallace glowing in the near distance. He'd converted a simple, nondescript, manufactured doublewide into his base of operations. It was practical, kept a low profile, and would be easy to write-off once he needed to leave town. His pick-up with the T-Rex logo was the only indication of the place being associated with the company. There were no signs and it was completely isolated from neighboring properties. Unfortunately for Liam, that was not a favorable arrangement in this situation.

We approached the building. Bern changed back into human form and tossed on just his shirt and pants. I started to do the same. "No need," he said in a low voice. "Stay off to the side as a bear. I'll be waiting for him in the yard. I need you to break a front window with your paw to get his attention and draw him outside. Then clear out and I'll take it from there."

A faint lighting emanated from the main room inside. Bern stood in the yard and indicated to me to smash in the window, which I did. It crashed loudly onto the interior floor. I hit another pane for good measure then bolted off back toward the edge of the clearing where I could watch the scene unfold. I wasn't sure if Bern simply planned to threaten Wallace, scare him, or start a fight, but he clearly was letting his rage build.

"You can't go burning down houses and killing people you asshole!" Bern yelled.

A porch light cautiously flickered on. Moments later, Wallace boldly emerged carrying a golf club. He was a big man, much larger than Bern. The type of fellow who didn't fear confrontations because he often had a substantial physical advantage.

"Who the hell are you and what do you think you're doing here at this hour?" he demanded.

"I know what you've done. Kate's death was no accident. Your goons just set fire to Hannah's house. And I'm here to make you pay for it." Bern stood motionless.

"Oh, is that right? I'm so sorry to hear about your poor honey's home," Wallace said mockingly. "It's a shame you're attacking me like this. I'll have to claim self-defense while an intruder attempted to break-in." And without further hesitation, Wallace charged with the club in both hands.

Bern had anticipated provoking him. In a moment he transformed, his clothes falling to the ground. Wallace hesitated and pulled up, not sure what he was seeing. In the same instant he was confronted with an angry black bear, standing on its hind legs. Wallace's eyes lit up like saucers. I could see his bewilderment from my secluded post. In a flash Bern was on him, clawing, biting, mauling. Liam Wallace didn't stand a chance.

Bern stepped off Wallace's limp body and changed back so he could retrieve his clothes, stuffed them into the bag, and we were off again as bears, adrenalin pumping, as we returned to the car. I couldn't register how I felt. I had just watched Bern kill a man, but I didn't feel remorseful. Wallace wasn't a decent human. He hired killers and divided communities, but did he deserve to die?

I carried those thoughts with me as we reassembled and got back into the car. "Sorry that it got ugly back there," Bern said, snapping on his seat belt. "Some people cross a line. Burning down Hannah's home was the final straw for me," he exhaled, calming down. "It's going to be a shit show up here once his body is found. We'll all have to be in hibernation for a while until the media circus leaves town."

We headed back to his home in Suttons Bay where Hannah was waiting. The events had all taken place so quickly. My head was spinning. Was I riding along with a murderer? Or were some people so awful that they deserved not to live? We're bombarded with the argument that lives matter. But do they? We've created gods. Invented purpose. Righteously proclaimed divine providence over a world inhabited by many other forms of life. But ultimately humans are a small blip on the cosmic scale of time. Perhaps it matters not at all. Maybe in order to keep a balance for the time being, Wallace needed to be removed from the equation.

We pulled into Bern's garage. The Westie was parked out front. Hannah was up, waiting for us. She didn't even ask a word when we walked through door. Instead she went straight to Bern and gave him a long embrace.

I broke the silence. "Looks like I'll have to find a new job. It's not like I'll be working the studio tomorrow."

13

THE CIRCUS COMES TO TOWN

The following morning Bern drove Hannah back to Glen Arbor to get her insurance claims in order. Meanwhile, Liam Wallace's associates found their boss dead on his front lawn from what appeared to be a bear attack. It looked as if he tried to defend himself with a golf club before being viciously mauled to death. There were tracks around the body, a broken window, yet nothing inside had been disturbed.

By the time evening rolled around the headlines were percolating on the news channels: *Fatal Bear Attack Reported In Leelanau County. Bear Kills Developer In Northern Michigan. One Man Dead In Fatal Bear Attack*. A bear attack was about as popular as a shark attack. National attention followed.

News reporters were being sent in from as far away as Boston to cover the story of the remote peninsula with little towns where bears lurked dangerously around every trashcan and corner. *These Woods Aren't Safe. Don't Hike Alone*. Videos and memes started popping up on internet comment boards. Cartoon Yogi the Bear stealing picnic baskets after killing the Ranger Smith. Smokey the Bear threatening you to put out that fire, *or else*. Replays of the grizzly attack scene from the movie *The Revenant*. And jokes showing the Chicago Bears with comments like "At least these bears aren't scary."

The next day, just as Bern predicted, the media carnival had arrived. Hotels, resorts and weekly rentals—already near capacity for the fall season—were now fully booked with the influx of reporters and a small but eager assembly of hunters. Michigan had select locations for bear season, but it sure as hell was not in Leelanau County. The hunters showed up nonetheless, using the opportunity as an excuse to circumvent pesky regulations, get a trophy kill, and perhaps gain some recognition on TV.

An impromptu gathering of clan members once again assembled at Dick's Pour House. Non-members, tourists, and local residents were turned away at the door, informed that a private party had booked the facilities that night. Bern had called the Sheriff once the media caught wind of the attack. Sheriff Roland was a prominent member of our clan and understood Bern's motivations. And more importantly, he agreed with his actions. He was the one who called the meeting to order.

Wallace had erred by stumbling into a united coalition invisible to outsiders. With past projects, his cunning tactics and deceit were usually successful, the lone exception being an endeavor in Florida where an adjacent retirement community of wealthy ex-New Yorkers opposed his development. Having little more than sunlight, crossword puzzles, and cocktail hour to distract their attention, those old folks fought to retain their ocean views and strolling access to the bank and pharmacy with a tenacity he never imagined.

And now the assembled clan members were preparing a cover-up for his killing because they all felt he'd asked for it.

"We need to get those damn media snoops out of here," of course that was Finn, "and make sure everyone in the clan keeps a low profile with those jackass trophy hunters waddling about. We don't need anyone getting shot."

"Finn makes a good point," Sheriff Roland's deep voice was booming. He was the sort of guy who could easily address a large crowd without the assistance of a microphone. "Let's spread the word to stay in hibernation until this story moves out of town.

Afterwards, winter will naturally bury the memory of it."

I had yet to experience winter in The County but to hear residents mention it, it sounded comparable to Minneapolis in terms of snow, ice and endless news cycles detailing the next storm front and how many inches of snow to expect.

"What can we do to hasten the media's departure?" someone questioned.

"We'll stage an event for them," Sheriff Roland said confidently. "We've had to do that sort of thing in the past. We need a volunteer for the cameras, someone to play *the bear*. My office will claim we tracked one down and positively identified it as the bear that mauled Liam Wallace. We'll invite some of our local connections to cover the story, get the word out, and we'll break the whole thing down in a matter of moments before any outside journalists can review it. The story will be aired on television. People will accept it as reality."

"I'll volunteer to be the bear," Bern offered. "After all, I brought the attention to us."

"Yeah, but it needed to be done," Finn amended. "You've been the noble knight who slayed the dragon that had been terrorizing the village."

"How will you claim to positively identifying the bear?" someone asked the Sheriff.

"We'll say it was spotted in the area of the killing, appeared aggressive—we will label it sick, diseased, mentally unstable— and after shooting it the deputies discovered blood still under its claws matching that of Liam Wallace," Roland summarized. "Case closed."

"Sounds like a plan. What time does the show go on?" Bern inquired.

"Let's adjourn and regroup tomorrow morning," Roland sounded as if he was conducting a board meeting for a condo association. "I'll contact the necessary parties later on tonight with the location and hour. It will be critical to be on time. We'll use a member's private farmland as the backdrop. We don't want an assembly of vehicles out in public that might draw the unwanted attention of a passing news crew or a bus load of curious tourists on their way to the wineries."

And with that, the threat to develop the land south of Leland into Lakeland Estates ended, and Liam Wallace was returned to Texas in a box.

***

After the "show" of Bern playing the dead bear, he met up with Hannah and I at the designated meeting spot. The others would already have broken down the set where they staged the photo shoot. We headed back towards Bern's home in Suttons Bay.

"How about a victory round at Hop Lot?" Hannah suggested. "It's a beautiful day."

Indeed it was and we all were in agreement. It had been a crazy week to say the least. A beer sounded good.

Hannah drove south through town and pulled into the unique brewery setting I had frequented often at the end of my biking runs. Hop Lot, as the name implied, was indeed just that. A year-round, open lot beer garden nestled among towering maples and cedars with a scattering of communal tables and fire pits. We placed our orders in the taproom and grabbed seats next to one of the campfires.

"Well, cheers to fine acting," Hannah toasted, clinking Bern's glass. "Do you suppose that we're finally in the clear?"

"I think so," Bern sounded tired. The sedatives he was under for the photo shoot were still making him mellow. "I'll be content to have a normal winter after everything that's happened this summer.

Well, I guess I'll be having you two living in my home so it won't exactly be the usual. But that's a welcomed intrusion." He added, "So Max, how have you enjoyed your summer of awakening?"

My prior life seemed exactly that—a totally different existence. I was a new person ever since the day I met Blue. I now met the mornings with a renewed sense of being. I no longer worried about things and events outside of my control. I was home.

"It's been awesome, in the purest sense of that word," I answered truthfully.

"When my home and studio get rebuilt, perhaps I'll amend the design to include a residential unit over the garage," Hannah was saying. "A Fonzie."

Fonzie was a character in an American television sit-com called *Happy Days*, set in the mid-1950s somewhere in the Midwest. He was the coolest dude in town, rode around on a motorcycle, always dressed in jeans, a white t-shirt and a leather jacket. His apartment was above the garage of a middle-class family. How cool is that?

Hannah kept describing her plan, "It will be the sort of space people have been converting into weekly rentals. But I'd be happy to rent it to you for a real deal, Max, if you'd still be interested in a convenient but independent location." Hannah's smile was subtle and her offer was more than generous.

I raised my glass in response, "Thanks." I figured I may as well push it, "Can you make it roomy enough for Lea as well?"

Bern and Hannah both laughed out loud at my bold request, but she didn't say no, either.

We sat there in the sunlight with the trees showing hints of the color explosion to come. "I'm starving," Bern said, finishing off his beer. "I'm going to get some food. Anyone want anything? Another round?"

121

14

A RETURN TO A BEGINNING

Weeks later October arrived and with it the changing season. Nights grew longer. The Big Dipper was lower in the sky. I found a job waiting tables at a restaurant in Suttons Bay. It filled the time. But my weekdays were open and I made trips to Lansing to visit Lea as often as possible.

One afternoon I decided to exercise the Westie by driving it out to the Clay Cliffs Natural Area north of Leland. The short hiking loop offered a walk through tall birch woods with a scenic overlook where you could see the Manitou and Fox Islands in the distance. Along the way I scared up a deer. The doe bolted through the woods effortlessly. No one else was on the trail and I entertained the idea of chasing her just for fun in bear form. Instead I walked out to the clearing and stood there overlooking Lake Michigan's majestic expanse of water. My journey to this spot seemed so incredibly improbable. But I could sense I was setting down roots for myself and generations to come.

I also felt the hairs starting to rise on my neck. I had that feeling I was being watched. The tattoo on my hand started to swirl in colors like the lake in front of me.

"Hello, Max."

I jumped like a frightened cat! Who the what? My skin was *crawling*. My heart, racing. I damn near pissed my pants. I hadn't heard anyone approaching.

Blue was strolling down the path toward me. She looked different. She didn't look like the false college student I met months ago in Marquette. Her dark hair was much longer. She was wearing tall hiking boots, jeans, a short black jacket, and a wide silver belt buckle with a bear's head on it. And her eyes were no longer green. Now they were a pale gray.

"Looks like you've come out of hibernation," she continued toward me, registering my complete panic. "Max, calm down. It's me, Blue. Really. You're acting like you're seeing a ghost." She stopped and reached out her hand, "Take it. I'm real."

I grabbed her hand and she pulled me in to give me a reassuring hug. "It's good to see you," she said into my ear, "and I'm happy you found our home."

I was speechless. I must have been as responsive as a tree. She stepped back to assess me, "Yes, you're definitely one of us now."

I finally snapped out of my shock enough to ask, "How did you?"

"How am I here?" she practically shined. Or maybe I imagined that. "Well, I'm making my rounds. I have— let's call it *a spirited means of travel*. You're one of my special cases so I wanted to see you in person before getting in touch with the rest of the clan."

"But how did you know I was way out here?" I felt like I was the only one on the trail.

"The Westie makes it obvious. I saw it parked in the lot while cruising along M-22," she was kidding but wasn't going to reveal her methods.

"Where have you been this summer?" I was coming around, returning to a normal heart rate.

"I was on an expedition to find our lost tribes. People like you. And others—" she dragged her toe across the dirt contemplating how much she wanted to tell me.

"Well, you wouldn't believe what's been going on here." I felt I had to bring my conversation up to her level. Never mind that I ever could. "I got to experience a Bear Lunar. We thwarted a developer from desecrating the lands south of Leland with a private golf course community."

She raised an eyebrow, "Is that so? Oh, I can't wait to hear about it. I need to call an assembly of the clan anyway. I just got back." She looked into my eyes. "And you. Did you meet someone? One of us?"

How could she do that? It was like standing in front of a mind reader. Maybe she was. "Yes, her name is Lea."

"Petra and Will's daughter? She's delightful. I love her *joie de vivre*." Apparently Blue knew everyone in our clan.

"What did you mean when you said you found other lost tribes?"

"Max. Well, you'll find out sooner or later. I may as well let you know." She looked out across the water, "After I met you in the U.P., I continued on through Minnesota, the Dakotas, and parts of Saskatchewan. I found no connections in the plains. It appears that stumbling across you was unique. As if I was meant to find you. You truly must have been from one of the lost tribes."

She gave me a heartening look.

"After the plains I searched the Rockies in western Montana, Idaho, and Alberta. That wasn't favorable. There are other clans; wolves, coyotes, ravens, grizzly bears," she paused. "Those grizzly bear clans are something else. Even I was challenged by *their* spirit bears. That long ago establishment of California as a Bear Republic was no coincidence. They're a powerful force out west."

I still couldn't quite believe she was there talking to me. I reached out and poked her in the arm.

Her face simply looked amused, "Yes, we've covered that already. I'm really here, Max."

"But how did you get out here?" I needed to know.

"I drove. My car is parked out at the trailhead next to your Westie," Blue said matter-of-factly. "As for tracking you, it's difficult to explain. I have a cosmic knack for that sort of thing."

I didn't pursue the question further and returned to her story. "So, are there other clans related to us?"

"After the Rockies I finally made it through Oregon, Washington, British Columbia." Blue went on, "Deep in the temperate rain forests I found remnant, isolated clan members, but none as cohesive and integrated into society as what we have here. They were outposts, people living way off the grid. They were of our origins but almost a different sect entirely given the vast expanse of time between us.

"I didn't expect much after that but continued on to Alaska, and it was there I really discovered a second home outside of Ketchikan and that entire chain of islands. I met with a wide organization of bear clan members who instinctively accepted me. It was a deep connection. I would liken it to someone in the America's discovering their roots, meeting ancestors from wherever they came from. Lost relatives from a different continent."

She paused and I didn't say anything. The wind ushered a new batch of leaves off the trees.

"I want to present to our Michigan clan a plan to reconnect with our relatives in Alaska. The introduction would be beneficial to both groups. They have conflicts to deal with as well and could use some help," Blue summarized, "but that's a longer story for another time."

"I can't wait to visit them." My mind was bounding around with the possibilities.

Before I could ask anything else Blue grabbed my and said, "Come on, Max. Let's go."

Paul Wcisel graduated from Indiana University in 1993 with a degree in History. Since then his work and life have taken him to Denver, Colorado, the District of Columbia, Traverse City, Michigan and Chicago, Illinois. He has held a variety of occupations, including: real estate agent, bank teller, gallery guard, barista, project coordinator, museum front desk associate, digital media editor, web designer, graphic designer, interactive designer, web developer, technical director, and now—writer. This is his first novel.

More about Paul and his artwork can be found at paulwcisel.com.